STACY WILDER

Secrets Are Hell

While Tim cocooned his body in the blue leather chair behind his desk, his fingers flew over the keyboard. The words flowed from his fingertips onto the computer screen. After he completed the final chapter of his novel, *Secrets Are Hell,* he leaned back in the seat that was positioned to optimize the view of the Caribbean. As he rubbed his newly acquired goatee, he watched the turquoise waves lap against the pearly sand.

When Tim and his former partner, Brad, sold their company, Multipoint Protection Services, Tim moved to Grand Cayman to pursue his dream of becoming an author. He grinned. His vision was about to come true.

After the identity thefts from his former company, Tim lasered in on the connection between the stolen information used to purchase prescription drugs and the subsequent laundering of the black market proceeds. The thriller was a product of his experiences, research, and imagination.

He recalled the conversation with his informant at the bar. Once the man he only knew as Jax consumed three shots of tequila, he'd spilled secrets about the money laundering business on the island. The man dripped sweat as he spoke, and he warned Tim to be careful with the revelations. Although Tim had fictionalized the facts gathered during his research, he prayed that he'd sufficiently disguised the characters involved in the illicit events.

Satisfied that the first draft was complete, he saved the document onto the flash drive and locked the device in the desk drawer. He stood and stretched his arms overhead before hiding the key underneath a leather-bound edition of *The Adventures of Sherlock Holmes*, one of many in his collection of books in the wall-to-wall bookcase behind him.

Tim raised his eyes toward the planked pine ceiling and contemplated his next steps. When he returned from Brad's upcoming wedding, he would consult with developmental editors. In the meantime, he'd let the story marinate. His phone pinged, and he turned back to the desk to find a text from his girlfriend, Becky.

Why haven't you called or messaged me?

His six-month-old puppy, Snooper, barked. He stepped away from his cellphone to let the dog inside. A salty breeze drifted through the opening. As he inhaled the scent, he wondered why he'd ever gotten involved with the former beauty pageant queen. He met her a few months ago when he'd volunteered at the rescue organization where he had adopted Snooper. While he massaged the black and white cocker spaniel mix's ears, he reflected on that day they'd both tended to the homeless pets.

As Tim handed Becky a bag of cat food, a jolt of adrenaline pulsed through his body. Becky measured the servings and filled the bowls they'd deliver to the felines. While she poured, he admired her flowing raven hair that framed a heart-shaped face. Her almond shaped hazel-colored eyes shimmered with intrigue. After he heard Becky's deep-throated laugh, he invited her to join him for a cup of coffee after their shift.

A month into the relationship, she began texting him incessantly. If he didn't reply within an hour, she'd get agitated. He regretted inviting her as his plus one to Brad and Liz's wedding in Charleston, South Carolina. A sigh escaped his lips. He longed for a soulmate like his friend had discovered in Liz.

Tim was delighted that the couple had chosen Grand Cayman as their honeymoon destination. He smiled in anticipation of the treasure hunt he'd planned as their wedding gift. Snooper wiggled away and bounded toward Tim's cat, Irish. The feline hissed and halted the puppy in his tracks. Tim chuckled, picked up his phone, and fingered a response.

Been working on the book. Meet up for drinks at five at The Deck? We can talk about travel plans.

Without waiting for a reply, he placed the device down and strode toward the kitchen to feed his pets.

Who knew that today would be the last time he would touch the manuscript?

Chapter 1

Dressed in my jammies, I sipped my morning tea and reveled in the few moments of silence before the wedding whirlwind began. Sunlight streamed through the kitchen windows. I prayed for good weather. According to the forecast, God had answered with a resounding "Yes."

As I nibbled on an English muffin slathered with butter and honey, I reflected on the last eleven months. Not long after I determined who was stealing identities from Brad's company, he asked me to marry him, and I accepted. While Brad negotiated the sale of his firm, he commuted back and forth between Charleston, South Carolina. and Carmel, California. Today, the incessant travel would end. We had agreed to live in Charleston and visit Carmel occasionally.

After we announced our engagement, my neighbor Lou and my mom collaborated on our reception. Lou, an interior decorator, envisioned a colorful flamboyant affair, while Mom fancied an elegant, classy event. Frustrated with my mom's refusal to consider his ideas, Lou quit twice. I begged him to stay, and eventually we all agreed on a simple spring-themed wedding.

When the wedding wars settled, the two of them became as thick as thieves. They'd been whispering behind my back all week. I dabbed at the perspiration at the base of my neck and hoped they weren't concocting some big surprise. The butterflies already fluttered fast in my stomach. I didn't need an unexpected turn of events.

By serendipity, my ex-husband had asked for an annulment on the grounds that he never intended to be faithful. The confession stung, and I thanked the Lord that I was no longer married to the man.

Brad claimed he didn't care if a priest married us, but I did. Although my ex had no regard for the sacrament of marriage, I considered the exchange of vows sacred. Our ceremony would take place at St. Michael's Church at six p.m., followed by a reception in our townhome community clubhouse. In less than twelve hours, I would become Liz Adams O'Connor. I smiled at the sound of it while my stomach continued to quiver.

My parents arrived earlier in the week from Florida. In the living room, my dad quietly read the morning paper with my Labrador, Duke, curled at his feet. You'd never know his only daughter was about to get married for the second time. No sign of Mom. I wondered if she was across the way at Lou's place finalizing the details for our reception.

A loud knock and a stream of barks from Duke interrupted my thoughts. I tossed the remnants of my breakfast in the trash and shuffled toward the commotion. Dad opened the door, and my neighbors Gwen, Cassie, Linda, and Maria rushed in and nearly bowled him over. My dog wove between them begging for attention.

"Where's your mom?" Cassie planted her hands on her hips. "The rental company is here."

"We have no clue where she wants the tables and chairs set up," Gwen added.

My dad interjected. "She and Lou left to run a few errands."

Really? At seven in the morning?

I sighed. "Give me a few minutes. I'll be right out. I'm pretty sure I remember where everything goes." I marched toward my bedroom and exchanged my pajamas for something presentable. The treasured few moments of silence had ended.

When we arrived at the clubhouse, I surveyed the scene. The community pool had been covered to create a makeshift stage, and the lounge chairs had been cleared. Outdoor chillers were strategically positioned in case the temperature became oppressive.

I instructed the staff on where to set up the rental tables to accommodate the forty-plus guests. They placed buffet and pub tables inside the clubhouse. When they finished the job, I inspected the space. I felt confident the layout was staged as planned. The ivory linens arrived just as the rental company departed.

I texted my mom.

Where are you?

Just drove up. Everything OK?

All good. Tables and linens are here.

Minutes later, Mom and Lou burst into the clubhouse. Beads of perspiration covered both of their foreheads.

"Where were you?" I asked.

"Oh, we just had a few final items to take care of." Mom winked at Lou.

If I didn't know for a fact that Lou was gay, I might believe the two of them had something going on.

"Doll, this is going to be the most amazing wedding." He inspected the linens. "Babs, do you think we should iron these?"

Since when did Lou start calling my mom by her nickname? That was typically reserved for my dad and her closest friends. My phone pinged with a text from Brad.

Have a few minutes?

Isn't it bad luck for the groom to see the bride before the wedding?

I have a surprise . . .

Be right there.

Brad met me at the door of the townhome, the one our friend Peg had left him in her will. The inside décor hadn't changed much, and even after a year of her absence, Peg's presence lingered. My heart squeezed, and my eyes misted with tears. I longed for her to experience this day with us. Peg had connived to get Brad and me together, so I hoped she was smiling from Heaven.

As I entered the living room, I inhaled the aroma of hazelnut coffee. French wing chairs flanked either side of the sofa where Becky and Tim sat sipping a cup of joe. I wasn't sure what to make of Becky. At the dinner we'd hosted to introduce our out-oftowners, I'd tried to strike up a conversation. Her answers sounded rehearsed, and she proceeded to gripe about their travels to Charleston. I eventually moved on to mingle with the other guests.

After I waved a hello to Tim and Becky, Tim stood and enveloped me in a hug.

"Love you guys," he whispered in my ear. "Thanks for putting us up. Can't wait to celebrate with you both."

"I'm so glad you could make it," I replied as I squeezed his shoulders.

Brad grabbed my hand and tugged me toward the garage. When he flipped on the light, I gasped. A white sprinter van with tinted windows was wrapped with a big red bow. I'd always wanted one for investigations. Brad raised the garage door to let the sunlight inside.

"You didn't."

"I did. Gunner helped me. It even has a bathroom."

"Wow."

Gunner was my ex-boss and mentor. When I first moved to Charleston, I'd worked for his firm, Bridgepoint Investigations, for a few years before I branched out on my own. I squealed with delight and leapt up to give Brad a kiss.

After I slid the door open, we climbed in. Camel-colored leather club chairs and state-of- the-art surveillance equipment lined the inside. Sure enough, there was a small bathroom with a sink and toilet. A mini-fridge and cooktop completed the ensemble. Everything I'd need for a stakeout. No more worries about holding my bladder until the job was done.

"It's perfect."

"Want to christen it?" Brad grinned.

"Ha." I playfully pushed him away. "We will, but later."

"I was only kidding anyway. I know you have a lot to do." As we exited the van, he sighed. "I wish my parents could be here."

Brad's parents had perished on Flight 93 on 9/11. "Me too." I squeezed his hand, then wrapped my arms around him and whispered in his ear, "Come with me. I want to give you your gift."

As we strolled across the street back to my house, I said, "I'm a little worried about Lou and my mom."

"Why?"

"Well, after months of being at odds with each other over our wedding, they're now besties."

He shrugged. "Don't worry. They're just having fun. Lou might have a future career as a wedding planner."

"True, but I sense something is up."

"Liz, relax. Let's enjoy our day."

When we arrived, Duke greeted Brad as if he hadn't seen him just yesterday. My dog and my future husband had a bromance going on. While Dad and Brad chatted, I retrieved his present. When I returned, my dad excused himself, and I handed Brad the small box. Tucked inside were vintage Celtic cufflinks. An emerald shone from the center of each white gold knot.

After he opened the gift, Brad grinned. "It's going to be a lucky day. Thank you." He cupped my face and kissed me. After close to a year, his kisses still touched me to the core.

My mom bustled through the front door. "Oops, sorry."

"Hi, Barb." Brad hadn't quite made the Babs club.

"Liz, honey, did you know it's already eleven?" My mom chided.

Yikes, I hadn't even showered, and I'd insisted on picking up my friend Sam at the airport. Her flight got in at twelve-thirty from California. Sam was the local sheriff in Carmel. We'd become fast friends when I'd visited last summer. My neighbor Maria had been kind enough to offer Sam her spare bedroom.

My hair appointment was at two, and I was getting my make-up done afterward. We were due at the church by five. I'd better hustle.

~ * ~

I spotted Sam as she made her way to the baggage claim area and waved. Her brunette hair had grown past her shoulders since I'd last seen her, and her face glowed with a California tan. Sam picked up the pace and strode toward me. I met her halfway and hugged her. Although we'd kept in touch, several months had passed since my last visit to California. "You look great."

"So do you, bride-to-be."

I glanced down at her rolling suitcase. "You have any luggage to pick up?"

"Nope. This is it."

We strolled out the automatic doors and across the lot to my Volvo convertible.

"Nice car," she commented.

Once we were buckled in, I said, "You'll never guess what Brad got me as a wedding gift."

"The suspense is killing me."

"A sprinter. It has a bathroom and a small kitchen. Wait until you see it." I rubbed my hands together before I placed them on the steering wheel and backed out of the parking space.

"I'm so jealous. We could use one or two of those on the force." She turned toward me and placed her hand on my arm. "Are you nervous?"

Sam knew about my previous history with my ex. "Like you wouldn't believe," I exhaled. "What am I thinking getting married for a second time?" *And what if it goes bust again?* I thought to myself and then said, "I know Brad's the right guy, though."

"Damn straight, but it's normal to have the jitters. It's your big day. I'm so happy I could be here for you both."

"How's Judge?" Judge was a bloodhound Sam had rescued.

"Great. Peanut's watching him."

"Peanut, the homeless guy?"

"Yeah, but he's not homeless anymore." Sam explained that she'd hired him as a custodian for the police station. Once he'd proven that he could stay clean from drugs, she offered him the apartment above her garage for nominal rent in exchange for maintaining her lawn.

"You're the kindest cop I know."

She cleared her throat. "Ahem, that would be sheriff."

"I stand corrected, Sheriff Sam."

"You gonna save a dance for me tonight?"

"You betcha."

~ * ~

The ceremony took place in the chapel at St. Michael's. In deference to Peg's parents, I didn't want to have it in the main church where Peg's funeral had occurred. Plus, our gathering was small . . . no wedding party and only Duke as ring bearer. The only other attendees were my parents, Peg's parents, Lou, Sam, Tim and Becky, Gunner, and Peg's niece Jenny.

When Brad gazed into my eyes and said, "I will love and honor you all the days of my life," the words pierced my heart and soul.

Tears rolled down my cheeks as I flashed back to my first wedding. Sawyer had stared at his shoes when he'd repeated the same vow. Had Sawyer intended to be unfaithful from the beginning? I cleared my mind of the memory and returned to the joy of the occasion. As I professed my vows, my heart swelled with gratitude for this wonderful man in front of me.

After the priest pronounced us man and wife, Brad kissed me with one of those toe-tingling kisses. We piled into horse-drawn carriages adorned with peach-and-cream roses to continue the celebration at Cooper's Cove's clubhouse.

While I surveyed the crowd at our reception, my mom gathered the long train of my dress into a bustle. The full-length ivory satin garment hugged my figure, but I might have to ditch the Spanx before the night was over. The compression on my bladder felt uncomfortable.

The invitations requested that guests dress in 'Bring your Spring, Charleston Chic.' The women wore pastel dresses with strappy sandals, and most of the men chose to wear a sports jacket with either khaki- or navy-colored pants.

I fingered the emerald necklace my parents gave me as 'my something new.' My strappy ice-blue mules encrusted with pearls were 'my something blue.' Peg's Aunt Jane had gifted me a pair of her emerald earrings for 'my something old.' Since my wedding band had belonged to Brad's mom, the ring counted, too.

Fairy lights flickered overhead. On the tables, vases overflowed with hydrangeas, peonies, and roses in shades of pink, cream, and lavender. My husband chatted with Tim at the bar. I admired the way Brad's dark-gray suit and starched white shirt fit his athletic body.

"Congratulations." Sam approached and then whistled. "You look beautiful."

"So do you." Dressed in a mint-green backless dress with her hair swept up in a messy bun, you'd never guess that she was a badass sheriff. I introduced her to my mom and then excused myself and sashayed toward my husband.

The scent of garlic wafted from a nearby chafing dish filled with shrimp and lobster pasta. Asparagus, carrots, new potatoes, crab-stuffed mushrooms, and the standby chicken warmed in the other pans. A vanilla and lavender wedding cake adorned with roses perched on one side of the dessert table. In honor of Brad's All World Athlete Ironman status, a three-tier groom's cake, decorated with images of each phase of the race, stood next to it.

Everything was perfect.

Lou rang a bell, a signal for the small crowd to gather for the wedding toasts. He grinned ear to ear as he commenced the celebration. While he welcomed the guests, servers milled about and offered each person a glass of bubbly.

Lou passed the microphone to my dad, and Dad raised his champagne flute. "Hello, everyone. Thank you for being here to celebrate my daughter's marriage. I promise to keep it brief." He cleared his throat. "We first met Brad on TV via a news channel. I'm sure most of you know that story." A few people in the crowd chuckled.

I cringed. My mom had not been happy that her introduction to Brad had occurred via a news clip gone viral when he'd professed his love to me during a chaotic triathlon.

He continued, "As we've gotten to know Brad, I couldn't have picked a better partner for our amazing daughter. Congratulations, Brad, and Liz. Cheers to many years of wedded bliss and continued surprises."

My mom giggled and then lifted her glass. Dad handed the mike to Mr. Kelley, Peg's dad, who read an Irish wedding blessing. Camille, Peg's mom, said grace, and then Lou declared the buffet officially open. Cameras flashed, and videographers recorded every moment.

After the toasts, Brad and I piled food onto gold-rimmed porcelain plates and then walked outside. The bride-and-groom table was located next to the make-shift dance stage. Tented calligraphy name cards identified each person's seat. My parents, Becky, Tim, Sam, and Lou completed our table of eight. Behind the stage, the DJ cued up instrumental jazz music.

Sam leaned over and said to Tim, "Liz mentioned that you're an author."

"I am." He beamed.

"What do you write?" Sam sipped her champagne while Becky glared at the two of them.

"Right now, I'm working on a thriller." As Tim expounded on the plot, beads of perspiration formed on Becky's forehead, and she rubbed the back of her neck with a napkin.

"That sounds like something I'd love to read," Sam said.

"I'll send you a signed copy when it's published."

Becky elbowed him and then whispered in his ear loud enough for me to hear. "If you say one more word to her, I'm going to kill you."

My mom raised her eyebrows. She'd heard it too. Other than Becky's looks, what on earth did Tim see in that woman? I wondered how long the relationship would last.

Sam stood, "Excuse me. I'll be right back." When she returned, she asked my parents if they could move over a seat, so she could sit next to me. My mom winked at Sam and then complied.

After we cut the cake, I escaped to the bathroom to wipe the remnants of frosting off my face. When I returned to our table, the DJ queued up Savage Garden's "I Knew I Loved You." Brad rose, and we swayed on the dance floor to the same song he played when he'd proposed. Next my dad and I danced to Lee Ann Womack's "I Hope you Dance," and then Brad and my mom strutted to Louis Armstrong's "What a Wonderful World." About halfway through the song, the recording scratched, and the outdoor flood lights went dark.

I gasped. What just happened?

Seconds later, disco lights swirled on the sidelines, while Brad settled into his seat next to me.

"What's going on?" I asked. "Where's Mom?"

Brad smiled and shrugged. The theme song from *Flashdance*, "What a Feeling," began to play. When the chorus started, Lou and my mom rollerbladed onto the stage.

Was my mom really wearing skates? I shook my head in disbelief as the scene unfolded in front of me. As they skated to the music, multicolored lights reflected off their matching long black t-shirts and flowing black pants. Video cameras followed every perfectly choreographed movement. I had a hunch this would be the second gone-viral video that I'd participated in within less than a year.

Before the song ended, the music stopped. While my neighbors held a folding cardboard screen in front of Lou and my mom, the lights changed to sweeping white spotlights. I elbowed Brad. "You knew about this, didn't you?"

"Maybe." He shrugged.

As they pulled the shield off to the side, "Putting on the Ritz" sounded from the speakers. Lou and Babs had exchanged the skates for tap shoes. While they tapped to the tune, I leaned over and said to my dad, "She's really good."

"They've been planning this for months, and she's been practicing non-stop since we arrived."

"So that's where she was this morning."

The corners of my dad's lips upturned in a guilty smile. When the song finished, Lou and my mom took a bow, and the crowd erupted with clapping, whoops, and hollers.

Gloria Estefan's "Conga" started to play, and someone switched the main lights back on. My neighbors formed a dance line. Lou and my mom high-fived and then began to drag people onto the stage.

When my mom grabbed my hand, I joked, "I think you just upstaged the bride."

"Sorry."

"No, really. That was amazing. Thank you." I kissed her cheek and then joined Brad and Sam at the front of the conga line, where I promptly tripped and upended the dance.

Sam helped me up. "Girl, you could stand to take a few lessons from your mom."

As we traveled back to our table, Becky poked Tim in the arm and then wagged her finger at him. I nudged Brad. "Becky doesn't seem very happy. Tomorrow's plane ride to the Caymans with them should be fun."

Not.

Chapter 2

After we boarded the private plane, I settled into the leather club chair next to Brad and across from Tim and Becky. In less than four hours, we'd be in Grand Cayman celebrating our honeymoon. I stifled a yawn. The party shut down around two last night. I'd be unpacking the memories of the evening for months to come.

If there was such a thing as a joy hangover, I had one.

When Brad first booked the trip, we'd planned to bring Duke. We secured the necessary paperwork and certified him as a service dog so we could take him anywhere on the island. After Peg's niece, Jenny, offered to watch him while we were away, we decided that bringing your dog-kid on a honeymoon wasn't the best idea.

A tall male flight attendant introduced himself as Jason and then took our drink order. I asked for a coffee, and Becky ordered a glass of champagne. She tapped at her phone and then held it up for me to see. "Eleven hundred views." She'd videoed my mom and Lou's performance. I couldn't wait to see the professional clip. As

Becky scrolled through her photos, she frowned and then turned toward Tim. "I asked you to take a couple of pictures of me. Where are they?"

Tim grimaced. "Sorry."

"And you didn't even dance with me." She put the cellphone down and crossed her arms. "*And* you talked to that Sam girl like forever. What kind of woman has a name like Sam?" The pitch of her voice rose a few notches as she stuck out her lower lip.

Tim shifted in his chair. I imagined that he mentally counted to ten before he responded. "Becky, these nice people are giving us a ride back to the Caymans on their private jet. Can we please save the arguments for later?"

"Fine." She snatched the champagne flute from the flight attendant, picked up her *Cosmopolitan* magazine, and took a big sip of bubbly.

I rolled my eyes at Brad and squeezed his hand. Tim stared out the airplane window.

The engines roared, and the jet took flight. Brad tightened his grip on the armrest. Brad's parents had perished on 9/11, and it had taken him years to overcome his fear of flying. It was the reason he mostly flew private.

Anxious to ease the tension, I asked Tim, "How's the book coming along?"

"First pass of the manuscript is finished. I'm ready to shop for editors. I want other eyes on it before I pitch it to publishers and agents."

I'd read a short story that he'd penned, and I loved his writing style. "That's great. When will we get to read it?"

Tim leaned forward and smiled. "I'll give you a copy while you're here. I'd like to get your feedback."

"Wow. Thank you. I can't wait to read the story."

"Take your time. No pressure to get your comments back to me anytime soon."

As Becky rustled the pages of her magazine, she murmured under her breath, "Really?"

The pilot informed us that it was safe to use our electronic devices. Brad released his grip and checked the weather. We were taking a chance with a trip to the islands at the start of the hurricane season.

"Looks like we might get a piece of Tropical Storm Bill." He passed the phone to me.

"As long as it doesn't turn into a hurricane." After I watched the radar, I handed it back. I whispered in Brad's ear, "Are you sure it's not Tropical Storm *Becky*?" I tipped my chin in her direction.

Tim said, "I hope it doesn't hit Cayman. Thunderstorms over the Caribbean are stunning. But, if they knock out the power, watch out. Traffic's already a nightmare. When the stoplights are out, it's a hundred times worse."

In anticipation of our trip, I'd researched Grand Cayman. The island was twenty-two miles long and at the most, eight miles across. With the overflow of residents and tourists, the drive across the terrain could take two plus hours on a good day. We'd decided not to rent a car. According to my research, taxis were abundant, and the public bus system was good. Plus, I wasn't enamored with driving on the left side of the road.

When Jason served lunch which consisted of lobster bisque and an avocado stuffed with lump crab, Becky perked up. "This looks yummy. Thank you."

While we ate, Tim shared his favorite places on the island with Brad, and Becky struck up a conversation with me. She talked nonstop about her experience as Miss Cayman. I was grateful when Tim interrupted her. "What's the name of that restaurant we went to for your dad's birthday?"

"The Breakers," Becky replied.

"Why don't we all meet there tomorrow for happy hour? Liz, I'll bring you the manuscript. Again, no pressure to look at it anytime soon."

"Awesome," I replied.

Becky shrugged. "Sure, why not?"

Brad added, "Sounds like a plan."

After lunch, I started to read the Sue Grafton novel I'd purchased for the trip. I nodded off halfway through the first chapter. My deep slumber was interrupted by the pilot's voice over the speaker.

"Folks, buckle up. Radar shows turbulence ahead. It's going to be a rough ride the rest of the way."

Brad clenched his teeth, and a bead of sweat formed on his forehead. I motioned for the flight attendant. "Will you please bring him a scotch before you buckle in?"

Jason glanced at Brad's vise-like grip around the arm of his chair. "I'll get him a cup, but it'll have to be plastic."

"Thank you," I said.

Becky screamed after the first bounce. I didn't know what was going to be worse, the turbulence or listening to Becky's theatrics. Her face turned green, and I prayed she wouldn't upchuck her food.

After a bumpy hour, we were finally wheels-on-the-ground, taxiing toward the airport. A golf cart waited for us at the bottom of the stairs. Brad had paid for a service to expedite us through customs.

As Tim led us to his car, Becky whined, "That was terrible. We could've *died*." The pitch of her voice increased, and she tugged Tim's arm. "You have to stay with me tonight. I don't want to sleep alone."

He put his arm around her and pulled her in close. "Of course, Becks."

Tim really was a good guy.

~ * ~

Our hotel suite boasted a king-sized bed, a small living room, a dining area and a bar equipped with a mini-fridge and microwave. I leaned over our balcony and admired the view of the Caribbean Sea. Palm trees swayed in the wind. The worst of the storm had missed the island, and sunlight sparkled on turquoise water. Last night we ordered room service, and we'd spent most of today lounging on the beach and recovering from the wedding festivities.

Brad wrapped his arms around me and pulled me into his bare chest. "Don't lean over too far."

"Don't worry." I rested the side of my head on his body and listened to his heartbeat. *Pure bliss.*

"We need to leave in an hour to meet Tim and Becky."

"OK. I'm going to take a shower. Care to join me?" I turned to kiss him. The glass-encased space, equipped with two rainfall showerheads, beckoned. My toes tingled in anticipation of a full week of kisses and more.

After our lovemaking, we traveled hand in hand along the shoreline toward the Breakers on Seven Mile Beach. My tangerine floral dress flapped in the tropical breeze, and my cheeks felt warm from the day of sun. "I hope Becky's in a better state than when we left her yesterday."

"Yeah, I feel bad that the turbulence spooked her."

"Um, not your fault." The white sand felt like powder underneath my bare feet as I swung my sandals in the other hand.

"It's weird. Tim hasn't returned any of my texts. Not like him." He extracted his phone from his shirt pocket and checked again.

"I hope they didn't get into a huge fight."

"Maybe he's just immersed in the book," Brad replied.

"I hope he brings the manuscript. I can't wait to read it."

We stepped onto the deck of the restaurant, and I slipped my sandals back on. Becky waved to us from a table facing the sea. As we approached, she took a deep breath. Brad pulled out a chair for me before he took a seat across from Becky.

"Where's Tim?" I asked.

"I haven't heard from him since he left my place this morning. I called and texted him. Nothing." She wrung her hands on the handle of her purse.

"You guys didn't come together?"

"No," she whimpered. "He said he'd meet me here." She dropped her gaze, and the volume of her voice lowered a few notches. "Um. We sort of had a fight before he took off this morning."

My PI instincts awakened. While investigating the thefts from Tim and Brad's company, I'd learned that Tim was obsessively punctual. He was officially fifteen minutes late. Maybe island life changed him, or maybe he was stuck in traffic, but something didn't sit right. "What time did he leave your apartment?"

"Around ten this morning. He said he was going to drop off his luggage at the house before he picked up Snooper and Irish from the vet."

A waiter dressed in shorts and a t-shirt with the bar's logo strolled up to take our drink order. Brad waved him away. "Give us a few."

"All tings criss. Let me know when you're ready." He moved on to the next customer.

"All tings criss? What does that mean?" I asked Becky.

"It means all good. We have our own sayings around here. It takes a bit of getting used to."

"Do you have the number for Tim's vet?" Brad asked.

Becky picked up her iPhone. "Sure. It's the same place where

I take my cat, Precious. I was glad she didn't have to be boarded while I was gone. My neighbor watched her for me."

"Can you please call and ask if Tim picked them up?" Brad said through gritted teeth.

Becky hesitated and glanced at her watch. "Yeah, sure. They don't close until six." She placed the call. "They're still there? Are you sure?" Becky held the phone away from her ear. "She's double-checking." After a few minutes, she said, "OK. Thanks." She placed the device back on the table. "That's strange. Snooper and Irish are still at the vet."

The wheels spun in my head. What were our options? We could contact the police stations and hospitals . . . or we could check out his place.

Brad voiced my thoughts. "Maybe we should go over to Tim's and see if he's there. I hope he just got caught up in the book and lost track of time."

"Yeah. But he said he was finished," I said. "He was supposed to bring me a copy."

"Maybe he wanted to do one last round of edits?" Brad replied and then turned toward Becky. "Can you take us?"

"Um. OK. I know where he keeps the spare house key." She cleared her throat. "I mean . . . if he's not home."

Brad left a note with the hostess in case Tim showed, and we piled into Becky's lime green Volkswagen Beetle convertible. The traffic crawled, and I was astounded by the number of roundabouts. After an hour, we finally arrived at Tim's place on the north side.

As we rolled into the driveway, I admired the view. Bougainvillea and palms framed a sprawling gray stucco home. Palm fronds lay on the ground from last night's storm. White shutters hung on either side of rain-spotted windows. As the sun set, a rainbow of colors reflected in the glass.

Brad rang the doorbell and rapped on the mahogany-stained front door.

No answer.

I peered through the beveled glass windows that flanked the entrance. "Maybe we should check the garage for his car before we barge in?"

"Good idea," Brad replied.

Becky hung back several steps as if she believed that someone might jump out from behind the fuchsia vines that bordered the building. Brad tested the garage's side door. Unlocked. Tim's open-concept black Jeep Wrangler was parked inside.

I placed my hand on the hood. Cold. "Is this his only car?" I asked Becky.

She nodded.

I strode toward the door that led from the garage into the house. Locked. Adrenaline pumped through my body as my PI training kicked in. "Let's peek in the windows before we use that key to get in." I didn't want to disturb a crime scene, if there was one. "Does Tim have a security system?"

"No. Most homes here don't have them. Even the estates. It's starting to become more of a thing, though," she replied.

The three of us wove our way around the perimeter of the

house and peered into each window. As we rounded the corner, I scanned the pool, surrounding patio, and state-of-the-art outdoor kitchen that faced the beach. We should be sipping cocktails and concocting plans for a barbeque instead of searching for Tim. *Where was he?*

Once we'd confirmed nothing looked amiss, we entered through the front. The unknowns that we faced were unsettling, and I'd feel more comfortable if I had a weapon on me.

"Hello," Brad shouted.

No answer.

As we stood in the entryway, I debated if it was best to split up or stay together. I opted for the latter. "Let's stick together and make our way from room to room to see if anything is out of order."

Becky's eyes darted around the space and then widened. She gulped.

Brad replied, "Let's do it."

When we entered the living room, I heard a scratching sound overhead and then a thunk. Becky shrieked.

After my heart traveled from my throat back to my chest, I whispered, "Where's the kitchen?"

Becky motioned to the left, and the three of us tiptoed down the hall. I withdrew two knives from the butcher block next to the sink and handed one to Brad. When I offered one to Becky, she refused.

"It's probably the bats. They've taken residence in Tim's attic. He's tried to get them removed, but it's a process."

Maybe . . . but I wasn't taking any chances. Brad led the way, and I tailed behind him, weapon in hand. Becky shadowed me.

We stopped in Tim's office. A large wooden desk faced French doors with a view of the Caribbean Sea. The dust-free surface was devoid of a computer. I slid open both drawers and discovered legal pads, sticky notes, pens, highlighters, tape, and paper clips. Everything an author might need. I checked the printer positioned on the bookshelf behind the desk. No paper. I peeked inside the closet. No sign of a computer bag.

As we entered the hallway that led to four separate bedrooms, I noticed a long depression in the middle of the navy carpet. I assumed it was a trail left behind by his luggage. Sure enough, we found Tim's suitcase in the master suite, waiting to be unpacked. Again, no sign of his phone, laptop, or computer bag. Maybe he *had* gone somewhere to tweak the story.

"Does Tim have a place where he likes to get away and work on the book?" I asked Becky.

She shook her head. "Not since I met him. He either writes here, or sometimes he joins his writers' group. They meet on Wednesdays."

I added, "Anybody he might have gone to hang out with?"

"Not that I can think of."

"I don't like this," Brad said.

I silently agreed. "Let's start calling the hospitals and the police station."

"Isn't that premature?" Becky asked.

"Not at all. If something's happened to him, the sooner we can start the search process the better," I replied.

After a stream of fruitless calls, we decided to quit for the night. The cops suggested that we wait a full twenty-four hours before filing a missing person's report. "Becky, will the vet let us pick up Snooper and Irish tomorrow?" I didn't want his pets to spend any more time locked up in a kennel.

Becky perked up. "I can get them. It's the least I can do."

I shot a quizzical look at Brad. "After that, can you give us the key?"

"Yeah, I guess." She shrugged.

"What was Tim wearing when he left your apartment?" I asked.

"A shelter t-shirt and navy shorts. I think he had on his tennis shoes." She hesitated as she thought. "Yeah. I remember him lacing them before he stormed out."

I fished a pen and paper out of my purse and handed them to Becky. "Will you please list anyone who might have information on Tim's whereabouts?"

She wrote down a dozen names and passed the note back. "I'm sure he'll show up soon."

After I tucked the information in my tote, I asked, "Tim has bats?"

"Yeah. The velvet free-tailed bats like to take residence in attics, and they're protected. Tim had hoped to get them removed before mating season. Once that starts, you have to wait for months."

Great. I sighed. This was not turning out to be the honeymoon I'd envisioned.

Chapter 3

The next morning, we caught a cab to the central police station in Georgetown. Brad tossed and turned for most of the night. We still had no word from Tim.

As we exited the taxi, I surveyed the area. The yellow, orange, and blue three-story building needed a makeover. White police cars with the RCIPS logo lined the parking lot. The Cayman British flag flapped overhead in the wind. The glass doors were covered in grime. When we approached the front desk, I spotted a familiar face chatting with the receptionist.

"JP?" I blinked my eyes a few times. It was either him or his body double. JP worked for the Directorate-General for External Security, otherwise known as the DGSE and the French equivalent of the CIA. He'd assisted me with my investigation into Peg's death while I was in Paris.

"Ah, the lovely Liz." JP met us halfway and kissed my hand. "You are part of the investigation, non? What a delight, ma chérie."

Blood rushed to my cheeks. "No. What are you talking about?" The base of my hairline grew damp. *This was awkward.* JP and I had a brief fling that I've never disclosed to Brad. After I informed JP that I preferred to be friends, we stayed in touch. Sometimes we consulted each other on cases. I'd failed to tell him that I was engaged to be married.

Before JP could answer, Brad stepped forward and cleared his throat.

"This is my husband, Brad," I said.

Brad extended his hand. Shock registered on JP's face, and he briefly hesitated before he accepted the gesture.

"JP helped me with the investigation into Peg's murder while I was in Paris," I added.

The air radiated with tension. Brad put a protective arm around me. I chewed my lower lip as JP answered my earlier question.

He leaned forward and lowered his voice. "The police commissioner and I are old friends. He's investigating rumors of money laundering on the island. Since the DGSE has reasons to believe it's tied to one of our cases, they've loaned my services to the investigation. What brings you here?"

"We're in Grand Cayman on our honeymoon," I replied. "But unfortunately, we're at the station to report that a friend of ours is missing."

We were interrupted by the approach of a man in uniform. He had a commanding presence, and his ginger-colored hair complemented his lightly tanned skin. "Righto, JP, I'll show you the way to the conference room." His British tone contrasted with JP's French accent.

Ever the gentleman, JP introduced us. "Liz and Brad, this is my friend, the Commissioner of Police, Aaron Holmes."

We shook hands with Holmes who had a grip like a vise.

"Aaron, my friends are here to report a missing person. Perhaps you could kindly direct them before we move on," JP added.

Aaron sighed. "If you insist." He marched to the front desk. "Adeline, please call Officer Henry to take a report." The young Jamaican woman picked up the phone.

"That's finished." He dusted off his hands. "A pleasure meeting you both." Aaron motioned down the hall. "Shall we go now?"

Before JP followed, he whispered in my ear. "There are secrets on this island. Be careful, ma chérie. Call me later."

We spent thirty minutes with Officer Henry. Brad and I described Tim and explained why we were so concerned. I provided the names that Becky supplied yesterday. There was no missing person's form. Henry jotted notes on a legal pad. He said he was sure Tim just had a case of island fever. I prayed that he wouldn't tear off the pages and toss them in the trash after we left.

"Care to fill me in on JP?" Brad asked as we exited the building.

"He helped me with Peg's case while I was in Paris."

"You already said that, *and* . . ."

Ugh. "We kinda had a thing while I was there."

"A thing?" His voice rose a notch.

I sighed, and a few seconds passed before I responded. "OK, I slept with him. It was just one night."

Brad stopped mid-step and stared at me. "Is there a reason why you never told me this?"

I dropped my gaze and plucked imaginary lint off my lavender cotton blouse. "We weren't officially dating at the time. I'm sure you went out with other people."

He considered my response. "True, but I didn't sleep with them the first chance I got."

I grimaced and put my hands on my hips. "What are you implying?"

"Nothing." He shook his head and then asked, "What happened?"

"My best friend was dead, and I was trying to find out who killed her. I guess I just got caught up in the moment."

As he mulled that over I added, "I told him shortly afterward that I just wanted to be friends. The whole time I was in Paris, I couldn't stop thinking about *you*."

Brad's face lit up. He grinned and then frowned. His eyes narrowed. "What did JP whisper in your ear?"

"He said we needed to be careful. Something about secrets on the island. Whatever that means."

"Hmmm." He studied my face.

Brad hadn't shown any jealous tendencies when we dated. Did he not believe me? My bafflement was interrupted when my phone pinged with a text from Becky.

Snooper and Irish are home. Key is under the back mat.

Thanks.

"Tim's pets are home." I released the breath I'd been holding, relieved to change the subject. "What's next?"

Brad studied the ground. "I'm worried about Tim, but I say we let the cops do their thing and try to enjoy the island . . . be actual tourists."

I frowned. "I'm not confident the police are going to do anything."

"Me either, but let's give them a chance. Maybe we can ask your *friend* JP for help." His voice dripped with sarcasm.

"That's a great idea." I ignored the caustic remark and fingered a quick text to JP. "Before we play tourist, can we check on Snooper and Irish?"

He nodded in agreement. "OK."

I kept the fact that I wanted to sleuth around Tim's place to myself.

~ * ~

"Oh my gosh, you're so adorable." I knelt on the kitchen's cobalt-blue tile floor and massaged Snooper's floppy black ears. Tim's cat, Irish, rubbed up against my calf. The cocker spaniel mix placed his front paws on my legs and licked my nose. "Who's a good boy?" The pup's tail swished as I scratched his back. "I miss Duke."

"Yeah, me too." Brad said.

I stood and sent Jenny a text, asking about our Labrador. "So now that Tim's pets are home, how are we going to care for them?" Becky worked as a bank teller during the week, so she wasn't an option. I needed to ask her about their feeding schedule. "Maybe the neighbors?" I offered.

"That's a good idea. We can also find out when they last saw Tim." Brad peered out the side window. "How 'bout I go speak with a few of them while you tend to Snooper and Irish?"

Normally, I'd want to hear what each person said and observe their body language, but there were drawers and cabinets that begged to be rummaged through. "Sounds good."

After Brad left, I made a beeline for Tim's bedroom, with Snooper and Irish in tow. A king-size bed centered the space. I unzipped the black hardshell suitcase on the leather bench at the end of the bed. Anchored in the middle of the gray geometric-patterned bedspread was an unopened suit bag. I'd check that next. Yes, I was invading a good friend's privacy, but it had to be done. We needed to increase our odds of finding him.

Soon.

In the luggage, tucked underneath his clothes, I uncovered Tim's calendar. I recalled that he preferred a physical calendar instead of keeping track of meetings and to-do lists on his computer or phone. As I flipped through the pages, my heart sank. He had a dentist appointment at two p.m. yesterday. A niggling voice inside my head said *I bet he didn't show.*

I moved on to the suit bag. Snooper tried to jump on the bed, while Irish swatted at him with his paws. I scooped up the puppy and placed him on the quilt. He sniffed the suit bag and whimpered. "It's OK, boy. We're going to find him." I rifled through Tim's suit pockets and came up empty. When I moved the bag to the side, I discovered an unsealed manila envelope on the bed addressed to me and Brad. I extracted a handwritten letter.

Congratulations to two of the best people I know. I'm so happy for both of you. Brad, you be sure to treat Liz right, she's a keeper.

I struggled to find the right gift for you both. After some deliberation, I decided it'd be fun to give you an experience.

Rumor has it, there's treasure buried on the island. I discovered this old map when I was sorting through a box of newspapers donated to the shelter. I thought it'd be a blast for the four of us to go on a treasure hunt. Ho, ho, ho, pirates, and all. Maybe we'll find some vintage rum.

Love you both,

Tim

I searched the envelope for the map. The only other document inside was a newspaper article. The piece elaborated on rumors of buried treasure and the history of the island's pirates, including the famous Blackbeard. The article was dated last month and alluded to modern day treasures and thieves of a wholly different kind.

"Liz?" Brad called from the hallway.

That was fast. "In here," I hollered.

"You're back quick." I scooped Snooper up and put him on the floor.

"Yeah, nobody was home on either side. What are you doing?"

"Searching for clues to Tim's whereabouts." I handed him the letter. "So, I guess this was intended to be our wedding present?"

Brad perched on the edge of the bed and scanned the document. "Tim said he had something he wanted to give us after we arrived. I guess this is it."

"There was a newspaper article but no map."

"Maybe he was going to add it later?"

"You're probably right." I held up the black binder. "I also found this."

"Tim's calendar. We need to turn that over to the cops."

"We will, but not until I've made a copy of it."

"Anything interesting?"

"He had a dentist appointment yesterday." A plan formulated in my head for retracing Tim's steps. I wanted to search for the missing map, but that could wait.

"I can see the wheels spinning in that head of yours. I'm just as worried about Tim as you are, but it *is* our honeymoon."

"Why don't I call the dentist? See if he showed up? Then I'll make that copy. We'll turn the calendar over to the cops, take a break, and try to enjoy the rest of the day."

"Let's visit Stingray City and spend some time in the water."

I longed to be an actual tourist. "Sounds great. Maybe Tim will turn up while we're gone."

~ * ~

The taxi fares were adding up. Brad negotiated a deal with the next driver to ferry us to the hotel for a quick change and then into town. On the way I phoned the dentist. The woman who answered said that Tim cancelled his appointment last week. I drew in a breath of relief. At least he wasn't a no-show.

We popped into an office supply shop, made a duplicate of Tim's calendar, and delivered the original to the station. I tucked the copy into my tote. Since Tim's letter and the article weren't likely related to his disappearance, Brad and I decided to keep that information to ourselves for now.

The driver dropped us off at our next destination, Ziggy's Tours and Charters. The hand-painted sign that hung above the shop door read, 'If it Zigs, it Zags.' A flyer on the door had an image of a boat and '*Discounts for Cash.*' Brad and I stepped inside to purchase our tickets.

A Black man in his sixties counted money behind the counter. Wooden shelves stocked with snacks, souvenirs, and
t-shirts lined the walls. "Sorry folks, last tour dun gone."

Brad's face dropped. "Well, so much for our first honeymoon tour in the Caymans."

The man grinned, showing off a gold tooth. He held out a calloused hand. "Name be Ziggy. How 'bout me take you two young 'uns on me own tour?"

Brad accepted the gesture. "That'd be great. We want to go to Stingray City and snorkel. How much?"

"Seein' it's your honeymoon and all dat' I only charge you five hundra fifty. Cash."

Brad handed him six hundred dollars, and Ziggy gave him fifty in change. He stepped from behind the counter, grabbed a cooler, and loaded it with beer and snacks. "Follow me. We gonna kick up rumpus." As Ziggy led the way out the door to the boat, he turned around and winked. "Dat mean we havin' a damn good time."

We climbed onto the motorboat and settled in the seats up front. The hum of the engine and the sound of the wake soothed my frazzled nerves. While the shoreline faded, I soaked in the sights. Motorboats, sailboats, and yachts bobbed in the water. Sunshine glittered on the blue-green sea, and a cruise ship floated on the horizon. Brad reached for my hand, and the tension in my muscles eased.

Thirty minutes later, Ziggy anchored in a spot away from the crowd of tourists. After he gave us a few safety tips, we slipped into the turquoise sea.

Careful not to make any sudden movements as instructed, I gingerly stepped onto the sand. A stingray gracefully glided toward us. "Wow," I mouthed to Brad when the creature brushed my side.

"Told yawl we's gonna kick-up some rumpus. Here, doll. Try dis." Ziggy passed me a long piece of squid. I held out the morsel and giggled when the wild fish suctioned it out of my hand.

Soon we were surrounded by the creatures, eager for a snack. Brad took a turn, and then we each hugged and kissed a large female stingray. Ziggy captured the magical moment on my waterproof camera.

"Dat bring each of youse seven years of good luck," Ziggy said.

"We could definitely use some of that," Brad muttered.

As the diamond-shaped creatures danced around us, the sun reflected off the sea's surface. After an hour, we reluctantly climbed back into the boat.

"That was amazing." Brad accepted an ice-cold Caybrew from Ziggy. "For a little while, I forgot that Tim was missing."

His words jolted me out of my short-lived bliss.

Ziggy dropped the can of beer he'd fetched from the cooler. "Who dat?" He grabbed a rag and mopped up the spill.

"Our friend, Tim Knight. He lives on the island. Been missing since yesterday. Do you know him?" I asked.

"Nevah heard of da man. Probably jes got da island fever." He averted his gaze when he gave me a replacement drink and then retrieved a beverage for himself. Ziggy popped the top of his beer and took a long swig. "Next we go to Ziggy's secret snorkeling spot. Discovered it afta da storm. Youse young 'uns gonna love it." He kicked on the engine and taxied us away.

We bumped through other boats' wakes before he slowed to a stop and dropped anchor. "We be 'bout a mile off Old Man Bay. Jes so ya kids know in case ya get lost." He winked. "A sailboat done cut loose in da storm and sunk. The fish are swarming down dere." He slipped a sheathed knife into his waistband. "Case we see any sharks."

I gasped. "Sharks?"

"Mostly nurse sharks. Dey be harmless."

Brad nudged me. "C'mon. It'll be fine. Look at the water."

The sand had settled from the storm, and the surface was

crystal clear. Not a single cloud drifted overhead, and gulls soared in the sky before diving into the sea for a catch.

"OK," I replied with more enthusiasm than I felt. We donned our snorkeling gear and slipped into the sea.

As we swam around the sunken ship, my mind started to whirl. Did Tim have a boat? Maybe when he got home, he'd ventured out to assess the storm's damage and had encountered trouble. Those thoughts drifted away as a school of angelfish swam past an eel. A green sea turtle paddled past the hull of the sunken ship. Coral swayed in the current, and a lionfish's mane of spines created brief marks along the sandy floor. Ziggy motioned that it was time to return to shore, and we followed him back on board.

"Did Tim have a boat?" I asked Brad once we were safely on deck.

"Yeah. He stored it at a marina near his house. He planned to take us for a ride."

"Might need to check it out." I tore into a bag of pretzels. I was starving.

Ziggy handed each of us another beer. He had a scowl on his face. Without a word, he grabbed a Caybrew for himself, turned the ignition, and sped back to the charter's dock.

As the vessel approached the shore, we both checked our cellphones. Reception had been spotty away from the island.

"Anything from Tim?" I asked.

"Nothing," Brad grumbled. "You?"

"Only a message from JP with an offer to buy us dinner this evening."

The earlier festive mood dissipated. Brad shrugged. "Why not?"

As I sent an acceptance to JP, my stomach clenched. I prayed this wasn't a bad idea.

Chapter 4

The cab dropped us off at Tim's house. After we took care of his pets, Brad penned a note and left it on the kitchen counter.

Sorry. Need to borrow your car. Call me as soon as you read this.
B

The Jeep came in handy. As Brad drove to the hotel, the breeze flowed through the open windows and roof. Back in our room, we freshened up. Brad changed into a short-sleeved white linen shirt and khaki slacks. I spritzed my favorite scent, Amazing Grace, on my neck and then slipped into a purple sundress that showed off my sun-kissed shoulders. JP had made reservations at the Grand Old House for seven-thirty. We'd take a cab into town, as I imagined the evening would involve a few bottles of wine. Tim's vehicle would give us the freedom to retrace his steps tomorrow.

The hostess ushered us to our seats on the patio. Brad had been silent on the ride over, and my stomach fluttered. Although I was starving, I wondered if I'd be able to eat. JP stood when we arrived. A bottle of Bordeaux was in a bucket next to him.

"Bonsoir, mes amis." He pulled out a chair for me, took his seat, and poured each of us a generous amount of wine. JP handed Brad a glass. "I hope you like a nice Bordeaux."

While I watched the sun descend toward the water, casting hues of pink, lavender, and peach across the sky, I prayed that JP wouldn't be as presumptuous about the main course.

Brad raised his eyebrows. He swirled the liquid before taking a sip. "Very, nice. Smooth."

JP raised his goblet. "Santé." We clinked glasses, and he asked, "Have you heard from your friend yet?"

"No. It's out of character for Tim. He should have called or texted by now. Have the cops made any progress?" Brad asked.

"I checked with the officer in charge on my way out today. I'm afraid he didn't have much news to share."

Brad crossed his arms. I could tell he was irritated by JP's answer.

An uncomfortable silence lingered in the air, then JP turned toward me and asked. "What happened with that insurance investigation?"

Two months ago, I'd phoned JP to get his take on a life insurance case I was working. "Turns out that the husband faked his death, and his wife was in on it. Thanks for the tip to keep an eye on her social media." After the insurance company settled, she'd friended a person who looked exactly like her deceased spouse.

"De rien. I'm glad I could help."

Brad flinched and accidentally knocked his fork off the table. He flagged down a server for a replacement. The edges of his ears were red.

Yikes. I guess I should have told him that I kept in touch with JP.

To break the tense atmosphere, I changed the subject and lowered my voice. "JP, you mentioned there were secrets on the island. What did you mean?"

The waitress interrupted, handed Brad a clean utensil, and then asked, "Are you ready to order?"

I hadn't even glanced at the menu. "I need some time."

"May I make some suggestions?" JP asked.

Uh-oh. Here we go.

Brad replied in a sarcastic tone, "Why not?" The tablecloth jiggled as he tapped his foot.

"I believe we'd all enjoy the ceviche of the day as a starter. For the lady, I recommend the lobster thermidor. And for the gentleman, the roasted grouper. I'm going to have the same."

Brad picked up his menu and handed it to the server. "That actually sounds pretty good."

I agreed, and the waitress went inside to place our orders. While I waited for JP to answer my earlier question, I swallowed a big gulp of wine.

"My apologies for being so forward, but I thought it best to get her out of the way so we can speak freely." JP lowered his voice to barely a whisper. I had to strain to catch his words over the ocean breeze. "Liz, the laundering is connected to the Corsican mafia." He leaned closer. "That's why the Commissioner asked me to help, and the DGSE agreed."

When I'd investigated Peg's murder, I discovered that Peg's Parisian boyfriend, Bjorn, had ties to the organization. From past conversations with JP, I knew he still lamented the outcome of that case. Despite the evidence, neither France nor the United States had elected to prosecute the perps. "That's interesting," I said. Maybe this time he'd get the crooks.

As Brad glanced at JP and then me, his eyes narrowed. I squeezed Brad's hand to remind him that he was my guy and then nodded at JP to continue. "Tell us more."

"Mais oui. Drugs are involved, and several prominent citizens are suspected. The body of one of our informants was discovered early this morning. Aaron believes . . ."

When the waitress approached with the ceviche, JP halted mid-sentence. "Merci," he said and waved her off.

Brad slapped the table, startling both of us. "That sounds like what Tim alluded to when he was in Charleston for the wedding. He said he was onto something big."

"Please, lower your voice. There are ears everywhere." JP surveyed the crowd to see if anyone had noticed Brad's outburst.

Brad groaned and shifted in his chair. While JP scanned the patio, I spooned shrimp ceviche with avocado, lime juice, red onion, and bell pepper onto my plate and ignored the mounting friction between the two of them. The growl of my stomach silenced my earlier nerves.

I passed the platter to Brad and then savored a bite of the tangy combination of textures.

Satisfied that no one was paying attention, JP continued. "We believe it's a sizeable organization. The investigation team is small, and we're keeping the details quiet. I'm sorry, but that's all that I can share at this point."

Brad stared at his plate. I imagined that he was processing what our friend might have gotten mixed up in. "If that's what Tim was writing about, he could be in real trouble."

"I'm afraid so." JP placed the ceviche on the table, his face somber.

"You mentioned that you and the Commissioner are old friends."

"Oui. We were suitemates at the boarding school I attended in Switzerland. We've kept in touch ever since."

Since JP's family had been in law enforcement, it seemed that he gravitated toward similar sorts. "Will you urge your friend to take the case seriously?" I asked.

"I promise I will do everything in my power." JP signaled to the server for another bottle of wine and then looked me directly in the eye. "If you try to find Tim yourselves, please be very careful and keep a low profile."

"We will," I replied for the both of us.

I closed my eyes and prayed that we'd find Tim alive.

~ * ~

"You didn't tell me that you kept in contact with JP," Brad said on the cab ride back to the hotel.

"We've remained friends. I like having other people in the business that I can talk to like Gunner, Sam, and JP. Is that a problem?" My voice rose an octave.

"I don't know."

"Well, you better figure it out." I crossed my arms over my chest. The driver glanced in the rearview mirror.

"At least *I'm* honest."

"Are we really going to do this? I didn't think it mattered. I'm sorry."

Several seconds passed before Brad responded. "Just give me some time on this JP thing." He put his arm around my shoulders.

I scooched closer.

Brad pulled me into his warm body. "I have an idea. Why don't we send the plane for Duke and Jenny? They can stay at Tim's, and she can watch his pets."

Duke had the ability to detect when people were lying. He yipped when someone wasn't telling the truth. His skills could come in handy. "That's not a bad idea. Ever since she hired Chantal, Jenny's complained that she's bored. I bet she'd welcome the vacation."

Jenny managed Peg's foundation for the homeless. After Peg's sister Chantal finished the rehab program that Peg had mandated as a condition of her inheritance, she'd asked for a job at the foundation. Sober, Chantal had established herself as a hard worker.

"Let's call Jenny," Brad said.

I phoned her and put her on speaker. "I hope I'm not calling too late."

"No, of course not. How's the honeymoon?"

"It's taken a bit of a detour." I glanced at the cab driver. He appeared to be intent on the road, but I wasn't taking any chances. "I'll explain later. How would you feel about joining us in the Caymans with Duke?"

"That would be amazing, but I don't want to be a third wheel. Are you sure?"

"Yes. We could use your help. Our friend had to leave unexpectedly, and we're caring for his dog and cat. It's kind of interfering with our honeymoon plans." I chuckled. That was the understatement of the year.

Brad chimed in, "I'll arrange a flight for tomorrow if that works."

"Wow, that's fast." The other end of the line was silent as she considered the idea. "A cheap vacation? I'm in! I think I can get everything worked out by tomorrow afternoon."

I added, "You'll be staying at our friend's house. Pack Duke's food and his leash." I explained where I'd filed the paperwork she'd need to get our dog onto the island.

"Can Lawson come?"

Lawson was Jenny's boyfriend. They'd been together for almost a year. He was an IT nerd and had assisted me with several cases. His abilities might also prove useful. Since he worked remotely, he could conduct business from anywhere.

"Of course. Bring him along."

Brad said, "I'll make the flight arrangements. We'll call you when we get to the hotel and give you the details. You have passports, right?"

"I do. I'm sure Lawson does too. How long are we staying?"

"Plan on a week." I prayed that would be plenty of time to find Tim.

"Awesome. Want to say hi to Duke?"

"Sure." I pictured Jenny holding the phone close to Duke's ear. Our voices changed tones as we told our dog that we missed him and said he was a good boy. My heart fluttered when Duke howled back an 'I love you.'

Once we were in our room and out of range of eavesdroppers, Brad booked the flight, and I mapped out tomorrow's plans to retrace Tim's steps. If all went well, Jenny, Lawson, and Duke would arrive around seven in the evening. Maybe I'd cook dinner for the four of us at Tim's house. When we phoned Jenny with the flight details, we explained Tim's plight. Perhaps all this would prove unnecessary, and he'd be home before the plane left the runway.

The following morning, after we reminded ourselves that we were indeed on our honeymoon, Brad checked his phone for an update from Tim. Nothing. He yawned, and I echoed with a sigh. It'd been another restless night. We piled in the Jeep and headed for the house.

Snooper greeted us, his fluffy tail wagging. "Wanna go for a walk?" I fastened his leash to his collar, and he dashed outside. We knocked on the neighbors' doors, but none of them were home. Since we hadn't heard from Becky in a day, I phoned her. She answered on the first ring.

"Liz, I've been meaning to call you. Have you found Tim?" Something about her choice of words bothered me.

"No. I assume you haven't heard from him either."

"Not even a text. But sometimes he doesn't communicate for days. Drives me crazy."

I imagined that her lower lip was stuck out in her signature pout. "Does anyone live in the homes on either side of Tim?"

"Yeah, but they're snowbirds. They're only here in the winter months."

"They don't rent out?"

"No." She hesitated. "They do have maintenance people. There are a couple of companies in town that manage homes while the owners are away."

"Anyone else in the neighborhood live here full time?

"There's an older couple at the end of the street. The large white house with the cobbled driveway. They have a sculpture of a dolphin in their yard. You can't miss it."

"Thanks."

"I need to get to work."

"Sure. Talk soon."

Becky hung up without a bye or a keep me posted. Either it really was always all about her, or she had something to hide.

"Becky didn't seem to be too worried about Tim," I

commented as Brad scooped Snooper's poop and placed it in a bag. I shared what she'd said about Tim's neighbors.

"Let's get the pets fed, and then we can stop by on our way out."

While Brad dished out their meals, I searched for clues to Tim's whereabouts. As I combed through his bedroom closet, Snooper bounded in and pawed my leg.

"Well, hello cute thing. You sure eat fast. Guess what? You have friends coming to see you." I scratched the top of his head.

Snooper grabbed my shoelaces and started to tug. "Someone wants to play," I laughed. He let go, barked, ran to the area rug underneath the bed, and tugged on the fringe on the far end.

"No, boy. Tim wouldn't want you to chew on that."

I bent down to wrench the carpet from his mouth, only to discover what appeared to be a secret compartment under the rug. Snooper sat next to me and licked my hand. I peeled the carpet back and then lifted the wood cover. In the hollow space below was a manuscript and notebook.

"Brad, come here." I shouted. "Bring Snooper a treat." At the word treat, his tail swished across the floor. "Good boy."

"What's going on?" Brad handed Snooper a biscuit.

"It's Tim's manuscript." Centered across the first page was the title, *Secrets Are Hell,* by Tim Knight.

"No way."

"Yes way." I handed the document to Brad. It was thick—at least three hundred pages. As I thumbed through the accompanying notebook, I said, "I think this contains his research notes."

"How'd you find all of this?"

I explained how Snooper had led me to the hidden space.

Brad perched on the edge of the mattress and read the first few sentences out loud.

"Secrets swirled in the island breeze. Some were harmless, like the sixteen-year-old girl who never told her parents that she skipped school to sneak off to a book signing event featuring her favorite author. And some could get you killed."

He set the story on the bed. "Damn."

We sat in silence for several long seconds before I spoke. "I don't think we should turn this over to the cops . . . yet. I'd like to read through it first." After all, this was Tim's dream. I couldn't imagine it being held hostage as evidence. "Let's go back to the hotel, put these items in the safe, and then retrace his steps."

"OK. Do you want to stop by the neighbor's house on the way out?"

"No. I'll feel better once this stuff is locked up." Even though I yearned to question them and then devour Tim's manuscript and notes, we needed to make progress while businesses were open.

Chapter 5

After the documents were secure, we drove to the Cayman Humane Society. According to Becky, today was one of the days Tim normally volunteered at the shelter. We parked the Jeep in front and strode toward the bright blue building. Inside, an older woman placed a cardboard box on the counter. Behind the reception desk corkboards pinned with pictures of pets available for adoption lined the wall. I heard mewling from inside the container. The receptionist handed some papers to the woman, who then moved to a side table to complete the documents.

"Is Tim Knight working?" I asked the woman behind the desk.

"No. He didn't show today. I've been calling and texting him, but no answer. It's not like Tim."

"We're friends of his, and we're worried. He's been missing since Monday," Brad said.

I peeked inside the box and spied a momma cat and six kittens.

"Oh no," she gasped. "My name's Wendy. Maybe you should talk to Leonard. He's the shelter manager." She swept her long strawberry blonde hair over her right shoulder and cradled an intercom to her ear. I caught snippets of the exchange. After she finished, she said, "He'll be out in a minute. Do you think something happened to Tim ?"

"I'm sure he's fine," I replied with more confidence than I felt. After we'd introduced ourselves, Wendy jumped out of her chair. "Oh, you're the couple that just got married. Tim spoke so highly of you two. Congratulations." She acted as if she wanted to hug us but instead shook our hands.

"Is Becky working today?" Since I'd exchanged texts with her earlier, I knew she wasn't, but I wanted to gauge her reaction.

At the mention of her name, Wendy wrinkled her nose. "Becky only volunteers on weekends. She has a job during the week." I gathered she wasn't a Becky fan.

The woman with the cats handed over the completed paperwork and a check. "Is that all?"

The receptionist reviewed the documents. "You're good to go."

A short, stout man, who I assumed was Leonard, entered the room. His hair was dark and parted down the middle. Silver wire-rimmed glasses perched on a hawk-like nose. Just like Wendy, he wore a magenta t-shirt embossed with the shelter's logo.

The man cleared his throat. "I'm Leonard, the manager here, and you are?"

"Friends of Tim," Brad replied. "I'm Brad, and this is my wife Liz."

"What can I do for you folks?" Leonard asked.

"We hoped that our friend Tim would be here." Brad's voice was thick with disappointment.

Leonard shrugged. "He was a no show. Happens with volunteers."

Wendy protested. "Tim is always here on his days."

Leonard ignored her comment and addressed us. "Are you interested in adopting a pet?"

"We're just visiting," I replied. "Maybe you can give us an idea of the work Tim does and show us around?" Something about the man's demeanor bothered me. His gaze darted around the room, and he hadn't looked me in the eyes once.

"Of course. Follow me." Leonard led us down a hallway. "I was disappointed that Tim didn't show up today. He's been helping me with a book I'm writing."

"Really? What's it about?" Brad asked.

"It's a thriller set on an island."

"Sounds fascinating," I said.

Leonard stepped aside and motioned toward a space lined with kennels. He raised his voice a few notches so we could hear him over the barking. "Like all our volunteers, Tim did a lot of different jobs, including walking and feeding the dogs."

Did he just speak of Tim in past tense? Maybe I hadn't heard him correctly. I stopped in front of a cage with an older yellow

Labrador mix. Sad brown eyes stared back at me. The label above her kennel said her name was Sadie, and she was good with kids and other pets. "What's Sadie's story?"

"Expats." Leonard spat the word out. "Got relocated and decided not to take her with them. At least they made a generous donation for her care."

Brad tugged on the sleeve of my blouse. Another minute in here, and I'd adopt them all. Next we stepped into a room stacked with boxes and bags of food.

"This is where people drop off donations. The volunteers sort through them and then stock the shelves."

"Everything's very organized," I commented. "How many volunteers do you have?"

"It fluctuates. During the summer when school is out, we have more. But on a regular basis, about twenty."

"Is Becky one of your regulars?" I asked.

Leonard tilted his head and smiled. He resembled a love-sick puppy. "Oh, yes. She's one of our best volunteers. Very loyal." The dreamy expression in his eyes faded, and he pointed to the right. "Here's where we store our medications, clip nails, and give the smaller pets baths. The larger dogs are bathed outdoors."

I scanned the locked glass cabinets filled with medicine and syringe bottles. My gaze settled on a stun gun on the countertop. "Is that a taser?"

"Occasionally a fight breaks out, and we have to tase a dog to break it up."

"Do you euthanize?" Brad asked.

Leonard sighed. "We try to avoid it if at all possible, but sometimes we have no choice." He changed the subject. "Over here is the cat room, and down the hall are the offices and the kitchen. Not much more to it."

"Thanks for the tour," Brad said.

"No problem."

I fished a card with my number out of my purse and handed it to him. "Will you call us if Tim shows up?"

He adjusted his glasses and then frowned. "You're a PI?"

"That's what I do for work at home. Here, I'm just a tourist."

He pulled his wallet out of his back pocket and placed the card inside. "Yeah, sure. I'll call if I see him."

~ * ~

Earlier I'd googled the locations of the island's marinas. Brad drove to the one closest to Tim's house. When we stepped inside the main building, a swarm of customers bustled inside the space, stocking up with gear for the day. Shelves loaded with life jackets, coolers, tackle, fishing poles, and an abundance of boat supplies bordered the walls.

We approached a man in one of the marina's neon green t-shirts. After he helped a family select bait tackle, he turned and said, "Sorry for the wait. Things have been a bit crazy since the storm. Lots of folks replacing lost gear and anxious to get back out on the water." He wiped his hands on his shorts. "How may I help you?"

Brad replied. "We're trying to find out if our friend, Tim Knight, docked his boat here."

"Tim?" I've called his number at least ten times with no answer. His sailboat was one of the ones the winds cut loose. No one's seen the vessel since."

"Is it possible Tim took it out?" I asked.

"Ma'am, you'd have to be crazy to take a sailboat out during a storm, and Tim didn't strike me as a loonie."

I shivered despite the heat. Was the sunken ship where we'd snorkeled Tim's boat?

Brad massaged the base of his neck. "When was the last time anyone saw it?"

"Tim or the boat?" He scanned the expanding checkout line. "Listen, who did you say you people are?"

Brad explained our relationship to Tim and our concern about his welfare.

He studied our faces and then seemed to take pity on us. "Name's Jeff." He extended his hand to Brad. "Our staff personally checked every vessel before Bill hit to ensure they were secure." He fetched a marina card and a pen out of his front pocket. "Here's Tim's slip number and the make and model of the boat, if you want to check it out for yourselves."

"Thank you," Brad said.

"You're welcome," he replied before he hustled off to take care of the next customer.

As we strode down the dock, I shared my earlier thought about the sunken ship. "Wasn't Ziggy's reaction to the mention of Tim's name kind of strange?"

"Not really." He handed me Jeff's card, and I used my phone to google the make and model of Tim's boat to see if it matched the half-buried vessel from our snorkeling trip. I shook my head and showed Brad the image, "I don't think it's the same."

"You're probably right. Although it's hard to tell for sure."

The inspection of the slip didn't provide any additional clues to Tim's whereabouts. The few folks on the dock claimed that they hadn't seen Tim since last week. Brad groaned in frustration. "If I find out he escaped to work on the book, I'm going to wring his neck."

I silently agreed, and then felt guilty. Tim's disappearance had spoiled our honeymoon, but what if something bad had happened to him?

Our next stop was the bank where Becky worked as a bank teller. While Brad drove, I jotted notes in my notebook. I missed the comfort of my home office, complete with whiteboard and corkboard. Often, as I pinned index cards and brainstormed ideas, the puzzle pieces would begin to take shape. Instead, I made two columns on the page and penned what I knew and didn't know.

<u>Known:</u>

Tim had been MIA since Monday morning with no contact.

His boat was gone.

His phone and laptop were missing.

He and Becky had a fight on Monday morning.

He didn't pick up his pets from the vet.

We had his calendar, manuscript, and research notebook.

<u>Unknown:</u>

Where was the map that he'd planned to give us as a wedding gift?

Was his disappearance connected to JP and Commissioner Holmes' investigation?

Why was he missing?

As I continued to add unknowns to the list, I wondered how I could narrow it down. While I put an asterisk next to the last item on the *known* list, my heart raced. Perhaps the notebook and manuscript would provide further clues.

Brad signaled a left and turned into the parking lot of Cayman Bank and Trust in Georgetown. When Becky shared her pageant stories on the plane, she'd divulged that the bank president was a family friend as well as her sponsor. After her post-contest funds dried up, he'd offered her a position as a teller.

Earlier I texted Becky and offered to take her to lunch. She immediately accepted and was waiting for us at the reception desk. Dressed in a white cotton blouse, black pencil skirt, and kitten heels, she embodied the stereotypical bank employee.

After she introduced us as her dear friends to the receptionist, we walked to her favorite lunch spot, Tropical Breeze. The sidewalk swarmed with tourists from the latest cruise ships. We stopped at the corner and Becky pushed the crosswalk button. She leaned toward me and whispered in a conspiratorial tone, "I can't believe Tim hasn't shown up yet. What are the police saying?"

"Nothing. I don't suppose you've heard anything new."

"Not since I answered your text . . . like twenty minutes ago."

She sighed.

The stoplight changed, and we stepped onto the street.

"Oh. By the way, we found someone to watch Snooper and Irish."

She stopped mid-step. "Really?"

The man behind her cleared his throat, and she increased her pace to catch up with me.

"I mean that's great. Who?"

"Some friends of ours. They fly in tonight, and they'll stay at Tim's place," I replied as we scurried to the opposite curb.

"But what if Tim comes home?"

Brad turned and said, "If that happens, I'll be more than happy to put them up in a hotel."

Once we were inside the air-conditioned restaurant, Becky gave her name to the hostess, and she led us to our table. Brad pulled out a chair for each of us.

As I took my seat, I asked, "How do you like working at the bank?"

"It's OK. Pays the bills. The teller business is tough on the manicure. All that data entry." She inspected her nails. "I like my work as a model much better. The Miami market is hot." Becky raised her head and batted her eyelashes at Brad. "Everyone tells me my lucky break is coming . . . I guess it just takes time."

Becky had to be in her late thirties. The clock was ticking on that career.

Brad ignored her flirtation and studied the lunch menu.

"Are you ladies ready to order?" He signaled for the waiter.

"I'm having my regular," Becky replied. "Caesar salad with shrimp."

After the server took our selections, a mahi-mahi burger for Brad, the conch chowder for me, and the Caesar for Becky, I asked, "Did you grow up on the island?"

"Born and raised." She grinned.

As I sipped my water, I longed for a Charleston-style iced tea with a splash of sweet. "Is your family still here?"

"I have a twin sister." She grimaced. "We're not identical, and she hates that I'm the island's beloved pageant queen. My parents . . . well Mom's a drunk, and my dad is always taking care of her."

"Wow. That's a lot." And more information than I asked for. I changed the subject. "Did Tim share his novel with you?"

"No. He wouldn't let anyone see it. I was surprised that he was going to give you a copy." She stuck out her lower lip.

"Not even his writer's group?"

"No. He did tell me he was ready to find an editor." Becky leaned forward and clutched the edge of the table. "Maybe that's where he is . . . meeting with potential candidates."

I recalled the conversation with Tim on the plane, when he mentioned that he was ready to find someone to help develop the story. I added 'review Tim's calendar and notes for any mention of editors' to my mental checklist. As I filled Becky in on our visit to the shelter, I studied her face.

She winced at the mention of Leonard's name. "He's creepy."

I dipped a piece of sourdough bread in garlic-and herb-seasoned olive oil. "What do you mean?"

"I've caught him staring at me more than once at the shelter." She paused and then added, "Like in a weird way."

I assumed she mentioned the last part because she was used to receiving looks of admiration from men. "Um, could you elaborate?" I asked.

"When I catch him staring, he gives me this awkward smile. And I swear I saw his car outside my apartment Monday morning after Tim left."

That was odd. "Maybe he was visiting a friend," I offered.

She shook her head. "I doubt it. He doesn't have many. Other than his three rescue dogs."

"What else can you tell us about him?" Brad asked.

"He grew up here. Everybody knows everybody."

I waited for Becky to continue.

"Leonard has worked at the shelter for like forever. He didn't go to university. Didn't have the money. His mom is a housekeeper at the Hilton," she explained. "His dad was a custodian at our bank. He died last year."

I brushed breadcrumbs off the tablecloth. "Does he have any siblings?"

"Just one. An older sister. She married a wealthy businessman when she was young and moved to Miami. Never looked back. Didn't even show up for her dad's funeral."

"That's sad," I said.

"Yeah. She's eight years older than Leonard. I didn't know her, but I've seen pictures. She's gorgeous."

Our conversation was interrupted by the arrival of our food. As soon as everyone was served, Brad bit into his sandwich. "Mmm," he hummed as he chewed.

I blew on a spoonful of chowder, inhaled the savory aroma, and then tasted. Delicious. The garlic-infused cream base had a bit of a kick from the island's Scotch bonnet pepper sauce.

Becky poured a droplet of dressing onto her salad and continued. "Of course, Leonard was in school way before me, but from what I've heard, he was a real nerd. His sister's popularity saved him from having like zero friends."

I was beginning to feel sorry for the guy. "Was Tim helping him write a book?"

"Leonard? Not that I know of. He's always reading on his lunch break, but he never said anything to me about writing a book. Tim didn't mention it either."

"What did Tim think about him?" I asked.

Becky's eyes pooled with tears. "He was nice to everyone. Even nerdy Leonard."

I noticed that she referred to Tim in the past tense.

Chapter 6

On our drive back to the hotel, the song "Vacation," by the Go-Go's played, reminding me that we were supposed to be on holiday. I stared out the window and watched the carefree tourists stroll along the sidewalk. That should have been us. Instead, we were on a mission to find our missing friend.

Brad interrupted my pity party. "If you make a list, I'll go to the store and buy the groceries for tonight's dinner."

I grinned. My husband was a dream come true. He knew that I hated the grocery store. "Deal." I squeezed his hand. "You're amazing." My heart swelled with gratitude.

Before Brad left to shop, we made love. After I handed him the grocery list, we kissed once more, and he set off for the store. I unlocked the safe and extracted Tim's story. Once I'd poured myself a generous glass of white wine, I slid open the balcony door, settled into a lounge chair, and grabbed the first ten pages. To ensure the tropical breeze wouldn't carry the papers away, I anchored the rest of the manuscript with a hurricane lamp from a nearby table. As I read his page-turning novel, my jaw dropped. The plot involved money laundering intertwined with an international drug distribution business. It sounded like the scheme JP had alluded to.

As I flipped over page fifty, a glint of sunlight flashed off the sliding glass door of an opposing condominium. The bright light caught my attention. I scanned the landscape and spied someone peering through binoculars pointed at our balcony. I scooped up Tim's story and scurried inside.

I took a deep breath and closed the drapes. After my heart rate calmed, I placed a call to JP. He answered on the first ring.

"Allô, Liz. How goes the honeymoon?"

"It'd be great if our friend wasn't missing. Any progress?"

"My deepest apologies. I haven't checked lately. I'll inquire after our call."

Why hadn't he followed up on our friend's missing person case? Did he resent my relationship with Brad, or was he too embroiled in the details of the investigation with Commissioner Holmes? My bet was on the latter.

"JP, I'm worried." I filled him in on what I'd learned about the plot of Tim's story, and about the person who'd spotted me while I read. Although the name of the island had been fictionalized, the descriptions of the settings closely resembled Grand Cayman.

"Ma chérie, you have cause to be concerned. May I get a copy of the manuscript? Perhaps it ties in with our case."

"Of course. I'll drop the story and his research notes off in the morning." Later I'd take the documents and the notebook with us to Tim's house where we'd join our guests for their first night in Grand Cayman. After reading the first five chapters, I didn't trust leaving them behind in the hotel safe. Although I longed to finish the thriller, I'd feel better when the originals were in the custody of the police.

"Did I offer congratulations on your marriage? Please excuse my manners if I did not."

"Thank you, JP. That means a lot."

As I ended the call, Brad opened the door. "Who was that?"

"JP."

Brad frowned and then asked, "Did he call you, or did you call him?"

Really? I thought as I stared at him.

"Never mind. Does he have any news about Tim?"

"No. Nothing." I shared what had occurred while I read the story and voiced my concerns about the contents of Tim's novel.

His brow wrinkled, and he paced the room. "OK. But that doesn't mean something's happened to him." He stopped and faced me. "*Does it?* And why is someone watching us?"

"No, of course not." I kept my voice calm despite his agitated tone. "I don't know why someone is spying on us. But my guess is that it's related to the book." I strode toward him, rubbed his shoulders, and tried to comfort him.

He glanced at his watch. "The groceries are in the car. Can you get your things together? We need to leave before the milk spoils."

As I added the manuscript, notebook, clothes, and some toiletries to Brad's duffle bag, I mulled over the situation with my husband and JP. How was I going to get Brad to believe that JP wasn't a threat to our relationship?

Another thought popped into my head, and I grinned. Soon, we would see Duke.

~ * ~

While I unpacked the groceries, I tried to relax. On the ride over, I'd vigilantly watched the sideview mirror to ensure we weren't being tailed. When we arrived at the house, the tension in my muscles eased slightly. My phone pinged, and I read the screen.

No new developments in Tim's case.

As I typed a quick response to JP's text, my stomach clenched.

Thanks. Keep me posted.

Irish wove in and out of my legs while I placed the ribeye steaks, ingredients for a mango salad, and an array of colorful vegetables in the fridge.

Earlier we'd spotted the neighbors that Becky mentioned as they unloaded bags from their Lexus. Once the pets were fed, we'd pay them a visit.

~ * ~

As we walked up the driveway of the neighbor's house, we passed a five-foot metal dolphin arched over a crested wave. Glints of sunlight reflected off the top of the statue. When we rang the bell, a woman in a flowing indigo silk caftan answered the door.

Her white hair was swept up in a bun. "How may I help you?"

Brad and I introduced ourselves and explained our relationship to Tim. "He's been missing since Monday. Have you seen him?"

"Not since last week. I'm Ida. Please, come in." She motioned us inside. "Let's sit in the living room. I'll get my husband. He's in the back."

In the lemon-yellow room, Brad and I sat on one of the two slipcovered couches that flanked an oriental rug. Ida returned with a physically fit man a few inches taller than her and a plate of cookies in her hands. "This is my husband, Neal." His ink-black hair appeared to be dyed. We exchanged handshakes.

"You have to try some of my key lime cookies. Please, help yourselves." She set the treats on the dark cherry coffee table.

My mouth watered as I picked one up from the plate. I could smell the scent of lime.

"Can I get you anything to drink?" she asked.

"Water, please," I replied as I nibbled on the concoction. Pure Heaven.

Neal took a seat on the far end of the couch. "I saw Tim's jeep coming and going a few times over the last couple of days." Ida must have told him the reason for our visit.

"That's us," Brad said. "We borrowed it."

"And I saw his girlfriend's car on Monday evening. Maybe she knows where he is? Ida has her contact information."

Another dead end. "We've already spoken with her. She hasn't heard from him either," I said. "Any other cars or activity?"

"We get a lot of traffic during the week. Maintenance people, housekeepers, pool cleaners. Some of them have logos on their vehicles and some don't. I could write a few names down for you," Neal said.

Ida returned with our water glasses.

I grabbed a second cookie. The buttery concoction was addictive. "That would be great." I fetched a pen and paper from my purse and handed them to Neal.

"We're very fond of Tim. He's a good neighbor," Ida said while Neal wrote. "Oh. Wait. You should talk to Pearl. She's the Cayman Marl Road Queen."

She caught my confused look and clarified. "Means she's the queen of gossip. If anything happens on this island, she's the first to know." She rattled off an address, and Neal added Pearl to the list. "Go hungry. Pearl's bound to feed you, and you don't want to miss it. She's a great cook."

We said our goodbyes, thanked them, and promised to keep the couple informed.

~ * ~

Brad left for the airport early. He claimed he wanted to allow plenty of time for traffic. I knew he was just as excited as me to see our dog. Although I wanted to join him, I stayed behind.

Tucked in a chair out of sight of any windows, I continued to read Tim's story with Snooper curled up next to me. Soon, I was immersed in the plot. An international cartel of drug dealers laundered money through the island's tourist businesses. One of the operations sounded a lot like Ziggy's place. There were plenty of shady characters in the book, including a prominent banker and a dirty cop. All lined their pockets with profits from the deals.

After ten more chapters, I couldn't stand it. I set the manuscript down and searched Tim's closets. He had to have a corkboard or a whiteboard somewhere. I struck pay dirt in the study. Tucked in the back of the closet was a flip chart. Hallelujah. I set up the easel, retrieved some markers and masking tape from a desk drawer, and wrote **Possibilities** at the top of the chart.

Disappeared on his own

Injured and unable to call for help

Kidnapped (ransom note?)

Accidental death

Murdered

As I wrote the last line, a hard ball formed in my stomach. I flipped the page and started another list, untitled.

Prominent Banker

Charter Tour Owner

Dirty Cop

After I listed some of the main characters in the story, I added Becky with a question mark. Although there wasn't a former beauty pageant queen in the book, her behavior had been off, and I couldn't pinpoint why.

I thumbed through Tim's research notes. He'd conducted a few interviews with experts in their fields but had only identified them by their initials. One of the sessions was with a banker with the initials 'SW.' I jotted the identifier next to 'Prominent Banker.'

The next section was titled anti-money laundering expert, with no initials, and included references to various governmental agencies and laws. According to Tim's notes, the Financial Crimes Enforcement Network or FICEN, a branch of the United States Treasury Department, collected and analyzed data related to money laundering from Financial Intelligence Units (FIUs) around the world. The agency in Grand Cayman was called the Financial Reporting Authority or FRA, and Tim had jotted down an address. I scratched my head. The page filled with acronyms resembled a bowl of alphabet soup.

Maybe Lawson could hack Tim's phone contacts. Another idea occurred. Perhaps I could coordinate the meeting dates with Tim's calendar. A quiver of hope surged through my body.

As I turned to a page in the notebook marked with a 'J.' Snooper barked, and I heard the garage door open. I hastily stuffed the easel and supplies back in the closet, pushed the manuscript and notebook under the chair, and ran to greet Duke.

Our dog slid across the kitchen's tile floor and almost knocked me over. I bent down, and he licked my nose. Duke and Irish had become fast friends in California, and the cat rubbed up against his buddy's leg. Snooper chased Duke's tail. After the chaos had calmed, I embraced all four-foot-ten of Jenny. "How was the flight?"

"I'm not gonna lie. Flying private is dope." Lawson scanned the space. "Nice place."

Snooper pawed Jenny's leg. "Everything was great." She knelt and rubbed his ears. "He's so cute." Her copper pixie caught a gleam of light from the setting sun. "Reminds me of my mom's dog, Bear. He was her constant companion during her treatments." Her eyes misted over. "He passed two months after she did." Snooper licked her nose.

Ovarian cancer had ended her mom's life when Jenny was in high school. "That's so sad," I said.

"Yeah. My dad said Bear died of a broken heart." She sighed and then stood and grabbed the handle of her suitcase. "Which way?"

"Follow me. You can get settled while I start dinner." I picked up her other bag and headed toward the larger guest bedroom. We'd take the smaller one. I couldn't bear to sleep in the master suite.

"I'll season the steaks," Brad offered. Duke halted at the word 'steak' and trotted back to join him.

After Lawson and Jenny found their room, I joined Brad in the kitchen and asked Alexa to play "Kokomo." Duke sat next to the counter while Brad seasoned the meat. When our dog heard my voice, he howled an 'I love you.' I gazed out the window as the sun set and cast shades of orange over the turquoise sea. The stress of the day's events lessened with the arrival of our beloved pet. Perhaps this trip could be salvaged after all.

I located Tim's blender and placed it on the white marble counter. While I chopped fruit for the salad and the mango margaritas, I admired the décor. Bamboo barstools lined the opposite side of the kitchen island, and matching globe lights beamed from overhead. Some of the white cabinets had glass doors with plates and glassware neatly arranged inside. As the blender hummed, the tune switched to "Who Let the Dogs Out," by Baha Men.

Lawson emerged from the back with Snooper at his heels. He'd changed into aqua swim trunks and a black t-shirt. Irish rubbed up against his leg. He backed away and almost tripped over Snooper.

"Do cats bother you?" I asked.

"Nah. They're OK. Just not my thing. I'm more of a dog guy." He pointed at Alexa. "I can get the search history if you want."

"Really?" Brad asked.

"Yeah, I'll do it first thing tomorrow."

"That'd be great." I passed Lawson a chilled glass of the frozen concoction and then extracted carrots, cauliflower, and broccoli from the fridge.

Jenny entered the kitchen. "What can I do to help?" She wore a long hot pink t-shirt adorned with sweeping green palm trees.

"Nothing. Cute cover-up," I commented as I handed her a margarita. "Why don't you two hang out by the pool with the dogs? I'm sure Duke would love a swim. I'll be out soon." Although I hated to spoil their first night in Grand Cayman, I added, "And I'll tell you what we know and don't know about our missing friend."

Brad and I joined Jenny and Lawson outside. While Brad placed the meat on the gas barbeque, I settled into the lounge chair next to Jenny and briefed them on the latest details surrounding Tim's disappearance and the discovery of his note about the treasure. We all chuckled as Snooper raced around the pool and barked at Duke as he swam. The puppy thought about getting in the water but placed one paw on the first step and then withdrew it. As dusk set in, the moon rose, and the stars twinkled in the sky. Snooper resumed chasing Duke along the side.

Brad announced that the steaks were ready, and Jenny helped me retrieve the sides, plates, and utensils from inside. The smell of savory meat drew the pups to the glass-top patio table. Over dinner, we agreed to comb through Tim's story and notes and then brainstorm ideas to find him. Tomorrow, Lawson would attempt to hack Tim's Cloud account. The knot in my stomach eased. I hoped the extra hands would help locate our friend. After we'd feasted on veggies roasted in coconut oil, salad with a mango lime dressing, and filet mignon, we retired to Tim's living room with full bellies.

Before I divided the manuscript among the four of us, I closed the blinds. I wasn't taking any chances after the earlier scare. Jenny snuggled up on the sofa next to Lawson. As I set up the flip chart, Snooper hopped into her lap. Duke curled up by Brad's feet. Irish took one glance at our dog's damp body and bolted toward the kitchen.

Brad handed Jenny and Lawson mudslide cocktails for dessert and then went to fetch our drinks.

"He likes you," I tipped my chin toward Snooper.

She patted his head. "He's just the cutest thing."

Lawson finished his first page and set it on the coffee table. "Man, this is some serious stuff." He ran his hand through his long dishwater blonde hair. Lawson resembled Shaggy from Scooby-Doo. Since Jenny had long idolized Velma, they were the perfect couple.

As we sipped our drinks in silence, I attempted to match the initials in Tim's notebook to his calendar. I found a 'J' and an 'SW' and marked the pages with sticky notes. Both entries had an address. I discovered a few other appointments with initials, but I was unable to link them to his records. When I discovered an appointment for a pest control company, I breathed a sigh of relief. A section of his notebook contained editors' names and contact information, but there were no corresponding meetings on his calendar.

A few pages in, Lawson interrupted the silence. "Hey, could this really happen?" He read a passage from the manuscript.

Miranda packed the shrink-wrapped packages of money into hidden compartments in her luggage. "Girl, this is so amazing. Free tickets to Grand Cayman and first class!" She did a little dance.

A member of a drug ring had recruited the girls to deliver the illicit funds from opioid sales to a courier on the island. Their four suitcases would contain over a million dollars in cash. The risk of getting caught was slim. The Denver airport had a reputation for lax security around checked luggage, especially for those flying first class.

Gigi zipped her bag. "The thousand in cash ain't too shabby either. I hope we can get more gigs like this. You didn't tell anyone, did you?"

"No way. It's our secret. I told my family and work that I was vacationing in Mexico."

What twenty-year-old didn't want an all-expense paid vacation to the Caribbean?

I googled airports with the worst checked bag security. Denver popped up along with several others around the world. "It's plausible." I shared the information with the group and then made a mental note to point out the passage to JP when I handed the manuscript over.

Two hours and another drink later, we finished. We should have been sleepy, but the energy in the room sizzled from the intensity of Tim's thriller.

I stood and uncapped a marker. Since I didn't want to bias the group with my earlier list of possibilities, I flipped the chart to a fresh page. "What do you think?"

"If these characters are based on real people and one or more of them found out about the story . . ." Jenny chewed her lower lip.

Duke whined, and Snooper raised his head from Jenny's lap.

"OK. Let's pretend that one of them did," I said.

"Maybe someone followed him home. Stole his laptop and cell phone, and then Tim went after them," Jenny added along her original train of thought.

Lawson interrupted her. "Yeah. But how do we know there aren't other copies? I mean if there are others out there, what's the point? Most authors have readers who help them with their story. If I was an author, I'd have back-ups of the story everywhere. How do we know Tim didn't?"

"According to his girlfriend, Tim didn't share his work. And I didn't find any flash drives in the house."

"That's odd," Jenny said.

"I agree. Worth investigating," I said.

"I'll check when I hack into his Cloud account," Lawson added.

I wrote 'Other Copies' and 'Cloud' on the flip chart, followed by a question mark.

Brad rubbed his chin. "That tourist business owner sure sounds a lot like Ziggy. Maybe we should pay him another visit and take Duke."

Neither Jenny nor Lawson knew of Duke's superpower. Fortunately, they were too wrapped up in our brainstorm session to question why we'd bring our dog. "There was a 'Z' in Tim's calendar but not in the notebook." After I'd explained who Ziggy was and how I'd matched Tim's notes with his schedule, I added his name to the list.

"What if it has nothing to do with the story?" Jenny offered. "You mentioned a buried treasure. Maybe Tim went to investigate and then tripped and fell. He could be injured and stranded."

That would explain the missing map and cell phone. "How would he have gotten there? His Jeep was here."

"Might be close by," Brad said.

I added Pearl to the chart.

"What's Pearl?" Lawson asked.

"Who," I replied. "According to Tim's neighbor, she's the know-it-all of Grand Cayman. If there's a buried treasure, Pearl might be able to point us in the right direction." That would save us a lot of time.

I heard a scratching sound overhead, followed by a high-pitched squeak.

Both dogs whined.

Jenny clutched her chest. "What was that?"

"I'm sorry. Apparently Tim has bats in his attic."

"That's so cool," Lawson said.

"Um, Lawson, so not . . . I hope they can't get into the house." Jenny shuddered and then yawned.

"I found an appointment for a pest control company on Tim's calendar. The creatures will be gone soon."

"That's a relief," Jenny said.

I tilted my head from side to side and tried to work the kinks out of my neck. "You two have had a long day. Let's sleep on it and reconvene in the morning."

I couldn't wait to pay Pearl a visit tomorrow.

Chapter 7

The morning coffee finished brewing, and Jenny poured herself a cup. "I never got a chance to tell you how amazing your reception was." She stirred milk into her mug. "I'm worried I'll never get married."

"Honey, you have plenty of time." After I set a tea kettle on the stovetop, I loaded croissants into a napkin-lined basket and then filled a second basket with fresh fruit.

"I'll be thirty in a couple of years," she sighed. "Most of my friends are already married. How did you know Brad was the one?"

"It was tough," I admitted. "My ex did a number on me. But I knew it was right when I felt a total sense of peace in his presence. How goes it with you and Lawson?"

"I think I'm in love . . . but he's so laid back. And he snores. How am I going to deal with that for the rest of my life?" She chewed on her thumbnail.

"Honey, everyone has their quirks." Including biting their nails, I didn't voice that thought. "You can always buy earplugs."

"Yeah. I guess. You got lucky. Brad's perfect."

"Did you know he's petrified of roaches?"

"No way." She giggled. "That's hilarious. Swoon-worthy Brad afraid of an insect."

Jenny followed me outdoors, and we set the food on the patio table where Lawson sipped a cup of joe. Brad and Duke swam laps in the crystal-clear pool.

True to his word, Lawson had found the Alexa device's search history. Aaron Neville sang "Tell It Like It Is," from the outdoor speakers, one of the songs on the playlist labeled 'Tim's Favorites' that he'd discovered on the device.

Snooper waited by Jenny's side for the next crumb to drop. Brad emerged from his swim, toweled off, and plopped down next to me. Duke shook and splattered water everywhere, and Snooper ducked under the table.

"You train every day?" Lawson asked Brad.

"Pretty much. My next Ironman's in Arizona. The terrain will be a challenge. Gotta stay in shape." He patted his stomach.

"That's cool. I might join you on your next run."

Brad shrugged. "Sure."

I tore off the end of a flaky pastry and dunked it in my hot tea. "Anybody have any grand revelations in their dreams?"

"Nope," Lawson said. "But I did discover some interesting things in Alexa's search history."

"Like what?" Brad bit into an apple.

"Like, how long does it take to walk to Mastic Trail? What's the best compact shovel for hard ground? What's the market price for antique gold coins? And an order for four night gear flashlights that's due to arrive tomorrow."

Jenny gave Lawson a puzzled look. "What's Mastic Trail?"

I slipped Duke a bite of bread. "How long does it take to get there?"

"A couple of hours by foot. It's about seven miles away," Lawson replied and then turned to Jenny. "It's a hiking trail inside a nature reserve. Loads of local birds and plants."

"Maybe that's where the treasure is buried," Jenny said.

Brad washed the apple down with a gulp of water. "Yeah, but why would Tim walk there? None of this makes any sense. What else did you find?"

"The usual. How long do you boil an egg? What's the weather? Nothing else stood out."

"So where do we go from here?" Jenny asked.

"I'll drop the manuscript off, and then Brad and I are going to pay Pearl a visit. You two enjoy the pool and the beach. Maybe the four of us can explore the nature reserve this afternoon."

~ * ~

Fresh from the guest room shower, Brad smelled like Irish Spring soap. I set my mug of tea on the table beside my chair and scratched Duke's back. As Brad changed into shorts and a t-shirt, I cleared my throat and said, "We're going to settle this once and for all."

"What?" He sat on the edge of the bed and tied his shoes.

My heart raced as I pointed at our dog. "Ask me anything and everything you want to know about JP."

"We agreed we wouldn't use Duke's superpower against each other."

"One-time exception." It was bad enough that Tim was missing. I wanted any insecurity about my relationship with JP resolved.

"OK." Brad rubbed his chin. "Was he good in bed?"

I rolled my eyes. Of course, a guy would ask that question first. "Yes, but not as good as you." No yip from Duke.

"And it was only one night?"

"Yes."

"Why do you still keep in contact with him?"

"We're friends. He's a great resource when I need fresh ideas on a case." I added, "You'd like him if you got to know him." So far I'd passed the Duke test with flying colors.

"Did you ever tell him about us?"

Ugh. "No."

"Why?"

"I don't know. I guess I didn't want to hurt his feelings." I regretted not telling them about each other.

Brad raised his eyebrows. "You weren't hedging your bets?"

"No. Damn it." I stomped my foot and crossed my arms. Duke whined. "What part of 'I love you and only you' do you not get?"

He patted the side of the bed. "Come here, boy." Our dog leapt up next to him and laid his head in Brad's lap. While Brad massaged Duke's ears, he mumbled, "I believe you."

Thank God Duke didn't yip.

He pleaded with his gorgeous aquamarine eyes. "Come join us." He patted the spot on the other side.

I cautiously took a seat next to him. "So, this is behind us?"

"Yeah. I'll do my best." As he shifted to face me, his eyes misted. "I love you, too, Liz Adams *O'Connor*."

"Why don't I let Duke outside?" I winked. "And we can pretend like we're on an actual honeymoon."

~ * ~

While Brad drove to Pearl's, I hummed to the tune that streamed from the radio, "Don't Worry, Be Happy." There was something to be said for make-up sex. I felt relaxed and ready for whatever the day held. Brad had even been cordial to JP when we'd delivered the story and notebook to the station and shared the details surrounding Tim's letter and the buried treasure. Although I doubted the authorities would deploy resources to conduct a search along Mastic Trail, I no longer considered the information irrelevant.

After we spotted Pearl's address painted on the faded yellow wattle-and-daub cottage, Brad parked in front. A couple of picnic tables framed the house, and chickens pecked at the ground. On the porch, a stout Black woman with a bulbous nose and long gray braids rocked in her chair. In the seat next to her was a thin weathered man with a bushy white beard. He was barefoot.

An electric fan whirled between their seats.

As we got closer, I smelled onion, garlic, thyme, and some other spices I couldn't place. My stomach grumbled in response. The woman, whom I assumed was Pearl, stood and smoothed her blue-and-white floral muumuu dress. "Hi, I'm Liz. A friend of ours told us about your place."

"I'm Pearl." She pointed to the man in the rocker. "This here is Jamaica Jams. We call him Jams for short."

I wondered how he'd earned the nickname.

As if she read my mind, Pearl continued, "Used to play in a reggae band. Course now he just an ole man," she chuckled. "What brings you to Mama Pearl?"

Brad explained the dilemma of our missing friend and his tell-all thriller.

"Well, 'scuse my manners. You folks come inside, and we'll chat. I just made a batch of my jerk chicken casserole."

"You better get some while you can. Half the island will be here soon." Jams winked.

"Why dontcha go home and fetch that guitar of yours? Show these folks how you can play. Heck, I may even dust off my tambourine."

As soon as Jams left, she said, "Dat way we can talk in private."

Pearl spooned rice and an aromatic chicken mix onto paper plates and then added a scoop of beans on the side. I could see how people would tell her their secrets. Her demeanor was warm and welcoming.

"Have you heard any rumors of missing people?"

I ingested a forkful of tender meat.

"Lordy, honey, plenty of people be missing. Tell me more about da story you said your friend wrote."

Brad expounded on the plot. "It's titled, *Secrets Are Hell*. A drug ring recruits young men and women to smuggle funds from illegal activities onto an island in the Caribbean. The money is then laundered through businesses and wired back to the crooks."

Pearl lifted her palms upward. She closed her eyes as if she were invoking other forces.

Brad turned toward me and raised his eyebrows.

"What's going on?" I mouthed.

Pearl's eyes fluttered open, and she shivered. "I feel bad juju. If what you say is true, your friend be in trouble. There are things happening on this island dat no one wants to talk about."

"Like what?" I asked.

"Like what you say. Dey be people washing money on this island." She shook her head.

"Do you know a man named Ziggy?" Brad asked.

She clicked her tongue and waved her index finger in the air. "Of course. Everybody know dat man. He crooked. He be part of it."

"Tim's story includes a banker and a dirty cop. Could those be real people?" I took a gulp of my water to ease the burn of the spices.

"Pearl no know for sure, but you may want to talk to dat cop, Dale Foster, and da banker, Spencer Webb."

She touched a finger to her lips. "You didn't hear it from me."

I extracted my notebook from my tote and jotted down both names. Was Spencer Webb the SW in Tim's research? I changed the subject. "Is it true that there's buried treasure on the island?"

Pearl narrowed her eyes. "Meybe."

"What about along Mastic Trail?"

She swallowed a mouthful of food before she answered, "Honey, dere be plenty of folktales." Pearl shared the history of pirates on the island and the rumors of buried gold. She grabbed my hand. "If you go, be careful. Dey say ghosts protect da treasure."

Brad used a napkin to wipe away the sauce that had dribbled out of the corner of his mouth. "Our friend Tim had a map, but it's disappeared."

After a moment, she said, "Find the iguana tree. Follow the parrot and stop when you find the turtle."

"What's an iguana tree?" I'd researched the local flora and fauna and didn't recall that species.

"How do we know which parrot or turtle?" Brad added.

Pearl rubbed her chin. "You'll know them when you see them."

As I contemplated her cryptic response, we were interrupted by the reappearance of Jams, with guitar in tow. Several locals trailed behind him, and Pearl stood to serve them.

"That was odd," Brad said.

"No kidding."

We followed the crowd outside and found a seat at one of the picnic tables. In a corner of the porch, Jams began to strum "Jamming" by Bob Marley and The Wailer's. A young man with Rasta dreads positioned a chair next to Jams and slapped an upside-down trashcan. A middle-aged woman tapped her foot while she harmonized with Jams. The joy on their faces was contagious. I couldn't wait for Pearl to grab her tambourine and join the party. After a few stanzas, I kicked off my sandals, grabbed Brad's hand, and tugged him to a clearing where a few people danced.

Three songs later, Brad pointed to his watch.

I sighed. This was what our honeymoon could've been like.

~ * ~

On the way to Tim's house, I checked in with Jenny. I placed the phone in speaker mode.

"Lawson found the map!" Her voice oozed with excitement.

"That's fantastic," I replied. "Where was it?"

"Tim scanned a copy of it to the Cloud."

"What else did he find?"

"A document with Tim's research notes but no manuscript. He didn't back up his phone or contacts. Lawson's searching for his cell phone provider. If he can, he'll hack in."

I had no doubt that he would. After I ended the call, I grinned. "I guess we're going on a treasure hunt," I told Brad.

Chapter 8

When we arrived at the house, Lawson showed me the map. As I studied the piece of paper, my pulse quickened. I could hardly contain my enthusiasm. "It's exactly like Pearl said! There's a tree marked with roots shaped like an iguana." Brad peered over my shoulder as I traced the path with my finger. "After we find it, we'll need to go off-trail and find the carving of a parrot and stones placed in the shape of a turtle." I pointed to where an X marked the spot.

Brad said, "Let me see."

I handed the map to him, and he examined it. "Damn."

"I can't believe we're going on a real treasure hunt," Jenny squealed.

"This is mind blowing," Lawson added.

When Brad passed the map back with a stern look on his face, my stomach dropped. I recalled the real reason for our search . . . to find Tim.

The four of us piled into the Jeep. Since Mastic Trail didn't allow pets, we left the dogs behind. Outfitted in t-shirts, shorts, and tennis shoes, we headed toward the path. The sign posted at the trail's entrance stated that the hike was five-miles long round trip. If the drawing was correct, in about a mile we'd discover a tree with roots shaped like a giant lizard.

We joined the other tourists on the trail. Lawson and Brad led the way. My tennis shoes squished in patches of mud, and the humidity was stifling. No island breeze wafted through the dense flora. The group in front of us stopped to snap pictures of emerald-green parrots perched in a nearby tree. On the other side of the path, a couple of turquoise-blue iguanas lounged on a large tree root. In front of us, a huge crab lumbered across the trail. Jenny grabbed my arm and pointed to a tree frog nestled in between two branches. I heard the tap-tap-tap of a woodpecker before I located the bird.

Forty minutes later, we found the spot. A group gathered in front of an enormous Mastic tree with massive roots shaped like an iguana. The tour guide explained that the tree was believed to be seven hundred years old. After the crowd dissipated, we headed off the path.

Lawson retrieved a compass from his pocket and pointed east. As we forged ahead, we scanned the area for a carving of a parrot on a boulder. We were careful not to touch any of the flora. The sign at the start of the trail claimed that some of the plants in the reserve were toxic.

Along the way, we searched the area for any evidence of Tim. Dead branches and leaves crunched under my feet, and an occasional lizard darted across our path. We could no longer hear the earlier crowd of tourists. Overhead, birds sang, and insects buzzed. My heart rate increased as we hunted.

We initially missed the small parrot carved in the limestone rock. When we determined that we'd gone too far, we doubled back and nearly stumbled upon the stone with the etched bird.

"Let's take a break." I mopped sweat off the back of my neck with a towel and extracted a water bottle from my backpack.

"Maybe we should keep going," Brad said.

Lawson studied the map and the compass. "Give me a little bit. I need to figure out where we are." He swatted a mosquito away from his ear.

Jenny squatted to rest on a nearby stone and then immediately jumped up. "Ouch." A jagged part of the rock had torn her shorts.

While she assessed the damage to her pants, I spotted a piece of purple cloth in a nearby crevice. "What's that?" I pointed at the ragged patch of fabric. It was probably nothing, but I retrieved it with the tip of my fingers and placed it in a plastic bag. The color resembled the hue of the rescue shelter's t-shirts. What if it had belonged to Tim? I stuffed the possible evidence in my backpack.

"I've got my bearings. This way." Lawson motioned ahead, and we all followed.

Sunlight streamed through the foliage and cast eerie shadows. What was Tim thinking, planning a nighttime treasure hunt? I was relieved that there was plenty of daylight left.

We stepped into a clearing where the vegetation was less dense. When Lawson spotted the rocks positioned in the shape of a turtle underneath a nearby tree, he clapped. "Bro, this is so unbelievable. What if the goods are buried under there?"

Brad rubbed his hands together, and Jenny squealed. I half-wished we'd brought shovels, but that would've been too conspicuous. Our mission was to determine whether our friend had been in the area.

"Maybe there is a treasure," Brad answered Lawson's question. "But we can hunt later. "Let's split up and search for any signs of Tim." After we each chose an opposing direction, we scanned the landscape for Tim. In twenty minutes, we'd return to our rendezvous point. If any of us found anything along the way, we were to text the rest of the group.

We'd almost completed our fruitless search when I heard Jenny shriek and the sound of a tree limb breaking.

Lawson hurried to her side. "What happened?"

"A snake!"

Brad and I rushed over. "Don't worry. There aren't any poisonous snakes on the island," I said.

"I know. I read the signs posted on the trail. But they're so slimy." She shuddered. "I can't stand them." As Jenny stood, blood trickled down her leg from where she'd hit her knee on the branch in her haste to get away from the creature.

Lawson handed her a tissue, then tossed the broken stick to the side and searched for the reptile. He brushed dirt off a small object and grasped it. "Look at this." In between his fingers was a gold coin embossed with a cross. He passed the object to Brad.

"Seems old." Brad turned the antique over and searched for a date. "Wow, 1715."

Lawson frowned. "Damn. That's ancient. Do you think someone already dug up the loot and dropped this?"

"Let's find out." Brad pocketed the coin, and he and Lawson strode toward the turtle rocks. They hefted the large middle piece to the side. The dirt was loose and darker in color than the surrounding soil. Upon closer inspection, Brad discovered footprints from what appeared to be a man's tennis shoe. "Appears so." He pointed at the indentations.

I measured the length and width with my arm, made a mental note, and then snapped a picture with my phone.

The question was . . . who?

~　*　~

Back at the house, we gathered on the deck to discuss the day's events. The dogs chased each other around the perimeter of the pool. Snooper had grown confident enough to follow Duke's lead and plunge in for a swim. Jenny and I sipped on a sauvignon blanc while the men enjoyed a cold Caybrew. I placed my bare feet on Brad's lap and begged for one of his world-class foot massages. My tootsies were tired.

A tropical breeze blew from the east, a welcome relief after the humid hike. "Day-O (The Banana Boat Song)" played over the speakers, another song on Tim's favorites list. My stomach growled, and I munched on a few chips from the basket on the table. I hummed along to the tune, excited about the evening's plans. Brad and I had reservations at seven for dinner at a restaurant in West Bay. I refrained from another handful of chips as my mouth watered in anticipation of the lobster dish I'd discovered on the online menu.

As we speculated on who might have uncovered the buried treasure, Lawson said, "My bets are on that boat owner you guys mentioned."

"Ziggy?" Brad asked.

"Yeah. That guy," Lawson replied.

"Could've been anyone. Maybe even a random person who followed Tim." What if someone had lurked in the shadows and then murdered him? Despite any signs of a struggle, the possibility remained. I sighed as Brad worked the kinks out of my feet.

Jenny tapped at her phone. "I wonder which pirate the treasure belonged to. Can I see the coin?"

Brad retrieved it from his pocket and passed it to her. Jenny's research skills were phenomenal. I had no doubt she'd find the source.

She grinned. "Maybe it's Blackbeard."

"That would be cool," Lawson said.

Our conversation was interrupted by a booming voice. "Allô." JP rounded the corner, followed by Commissioner Holmes. They stepped onto the patio and halted side by side in front of the table.

Jenny placed the coin underneath her phone, and I extracted my feet from Brad's lap.

JP's gaze settled on Jenny and then Lawson. "I apologize for the intrusion."

My stomach twisted. What were they doing here?

Brad introduced our friends. The pups emerged from the pool and rushed to greet the visitors.

I gasped when Duke shook water all over Commissioner Holmes. "I'm so sorry."

"Righto . . . Not a problem. Anyone have a towel?"

Brad handed a fresh beach towel to the police officer and then dried off Snooper and Duke. The dogs' antics broke the serious mood that hung in the air.

"This must be Duke." JP patted my dog on the head.

I nodded. He probably recognized him from the picture I'd shown him in Paris. I glanced at Brad. He seemed unfazed by JP's comment and focused on the unexpected appearance of the two of them.

After Commissioner Holmes toweled off his uniform, he took charge. "I'm afraid I have some bad news. Is it OK for your friends to be present?"

I closed my eyes to banish the image of the policeman's somber face. My heart sank. I wasn't sure I wanted to hear what he was about to say.

"Yes. Go ahead," Brad said.

The commissioner continued, "Some divers discovered a body offshore. We believe it may be Tim's."

JP lowered his gaze. "I'm sorry."

"Oh no," Jenny gasped.

"Damn," Lawson said.

Brad slumped in his chair, and I reached for his hand.

"How do you know it's Tim?" I asked.

"We're not positive. But the body matches the description you provided. We'd like to have someone identify the corpse. I must warn you. It will be difficult. The sharks . . ." Commissioner Holmes cleared his throat.

My vision blurred, and I blinked my eyes until Aaron's face came into focus.

"I'll go," Brad groaned. Duke whined and then placed his head on Brad's lap. "Give me a few minutes to change."

"I'm coming with you." I stood on shaky legs.

Jenny held on to Duke's collar. "We'll watch the pets," she said. Her topaz-colored eyes radiated concern.

Back in the guest room, Brad exchanged his sweat-soaked t-shirt for a fresh polo. "You don't have to go."

"Nonsense. Of course, I'm coming with you."

"It's not like I haven't seen a dead body before."

Was he referring to his younger sister who drowned in their pool when he was a teenager?

He peeled off his muddy shorts, slipped on a clean pair, and sat on the edge of the bed. "Liz," he groaned. "I don't know if this is going to work."

I dropped the clean t-shirt I had in my hand. "What are you talking about?" My voice rose a few notches.

"Us." He frowned. "This honeymoon is a disaster. I'm a curse. My sister, my parents, Peg, and now Tim."

He rubbed the back of his neck. "You deserve better."

My legs felt wobbly. I crossed my arms and glared at him. Tears streamed down my face. I struggled for words and then found my voice. "So, this is all *your* fault, *right*? And my baby dying in utero was *my* fault." My outrage built, and by the end I was yelling. "And my best friend Peg's death was *my* fault, and now Tim is *my* fault."

The silence that followed vibrated in the room. My heart pounded in my chest, and I wiped my damp eyes with the back of my hand.

After moments that seemed like hours, Brad put his elbows on his knees and sunk his forehead into his palms. "I'm sorry. It's just that I couldn't stand it if something happened to you."

I sighed a deep breath of relief and plopped down next to him. As I draped my arm over his shoulder, I whispered in his ear, "Brad O'Connor, I don't care if I have one minute left in this world or a hundred years. I want to spend every bit as your wife. Did you not hear me this morning? I love you."

He wrapped his arms around me and then responded. "I don't deserve you, but I'll do my best. I love you too." We held each other tight and gathered strength for what lay ahead. Brad said, "I guess we better get going."

Yep, this was the honeymoon from hell.

Chapter 9

My stomach churned from what we'd witnessed in the morgue. Although I'd seen my fair share of dead bodies, I'd never had to identify one that had been shark bait. The small quill tattoo on Tim's left ankle had remained intact and left no doubt that it was him. Tim had the symbol etched on his leg to commemorate his new career as an author. One that had been cruelly cut short.

As we waited in the conference room for Commissioner Holmes, I rubbed my arms and attempted to ward off the chill in the air.

Brad's face was ashen.

"Are you OK?" I asked. It was a stupid question. He wasn't alright, and neither was I.

"I guess I'll need to call his brother."

The tasks were overwhelming . . . sign paperwork, notify the family, help them plan a funeral.

Find the murderer.

Before the commissioner took his seat at the long pine table, he asked, "May I get you folks something to drink? A water?"

"Or perhaps something stronger?" JP added.

Brad shook his head, and I voiced a reply for both of us, "No, thank you. If we could please get on with it."

"Righto. First off, I'm very sorry for the unfortunate circumstances. You can be assured that this case is a priority, and please call me Aaron." He hesitated and then continued. "I have a few questions and then some documents for you to sign. The coroner will conduct a full autopsy." He added, "And we're keeping his death out of the news for now. I'd appreciate it if you and your friends would refrain from discussing the details with anyone else on the island."

"OK. I'll need to notify his brother. He's in California," Brad said.

"Of course," Aaron replied. "Anyone else?"

"Tim's lawyer lives on the island. I'll need to contact him too since I'm the executor of Tim's estate."

JP and Aaron glanced at each other.

I kept my mouth shut. After they researched Brad's net worth, they would realize he had no motive to kill his friend.

Once we'd answered questions about our arrival in the Caymans and our subsequent search for Tim, Brad signed the forms. "Are we free to go now?"

The clock on the wall read seven thirty, way past our dinner reservations.

I wasn't sure I'd be able to stomach anything anyway. I longed to curl up in Brad's arms and cry.

"Actually, JP and I have business that we'd like to discuss with Liz," Aaron replied.

As Brad stood to leave the room, I grabbed his hand. "Anything you want to talk to me about will need to be with Brad present."

"Very well. JP, tell Liz about our proposal."

JP cleared his throat. "I realize this is your honeymoon . . ."

"A wrecked one," Brad interjected.

"Liz, we'd like to add you to our investigation team. Strictly as a consultant with a focus on the connection that Tim's death may have to the broader case." JP paused to let the words sink in.

The commissioner filled in the silence. "Of course, you'd be paid. I've already cleared the work visa, as well as a handgun temporarily registered in your name." He added, "I realize you've had quite the shock. Please take some time to think about it."

I was flabbergasted by the offer and how fast they'd put the details together.

Aaron continued, "You'll have full access to the department's files and equipment."

"Liz, it's a good idea," Brad said.

My mind whirled. Brad appeared to be OK around JP, but how would he react if I worked alongside a former fling? And did I have it in me to pursue yet another case that was so deeply personal?

JP added, "Tim's murder takes this to a new level of danger. As part of the investigation team, you will also have increased protection. Both of you. And your friends."

I gazed at the French manicure that I'd gotten over a week ago . . . before this nightmare happened . . . when I'd joyfully anticipated our wedding. "What would be expected of me?"

Aaron answered, "We meet every morning at eight a.m. sharp to review reports and the previous day's events. Then we discuss the plans for the day and adjust accordingly. You'd be expected to join us, although you'd have some leverage on what assignments you take around the investigation into Tim's death." He shrugged. "Given that it's your honeymoon and all."

I groaned. "Can I join via phone?" I dreaded driving to the station on the wrong side of the road in heavy traffic.

After a moment, he conceded. "I suppose." He gave JP a look that I interpreted as *is she always this difficult?*

"Can Brad come along on some of the assignments?"

"Not in an official capacity. But if he happens to be where you are, I don't have a problem with it. You?" he asked JP.

"Fine by me."

"Let me sleep on it," I said. But I already knew the answer was yes.

~ * ~

On the way from the station to our hotel, I phoned Jenny to let her know the forensics team was headed to Tim's house. "You'll need to be outside while they work. It's going to be dusty. When they're finished, you can pick a room to stay in. The police will send a clean-up crew to tidy the rest of the house first thing in the morning."

"I've never been a part of a crime scene. What about Irish?" Jenny asked.

"I saw a couple of cat carriers in the garage. Place him in one and take him outside with you." I had a feeling that would be easier said than done.

"Good idea." She took a deep breath and then asked, "How are you guys doing?"

I glanced at Brad's ashen face. "Not good. This sucks . . . but we'll get through it."

"Let me know if I can do anything. Call or text me. I don't care what time it is."

"Thanks, Jenny. I'm sorry you and Lawson are having to deal with this. I love you."

"No need to apologize. I love you too, Liz. Give Brad a big hug from me."

After we'd settled in our room, Brad called Tim's older brother, Jim, and broke the news. Before the call ended, Brad assured Jim that he'd research possible funeral homes tomorrow.

Once Brad hung up, he plopped down on the bed. He explained that as soon as Tim's body was released, he'd be cremated. There would be an initial service in the Caymans, and then his ashes would be flown to his hometown in California where a memorial service would be held. Tim had arranged in advance for his remains to be buried in the family plot next to both of his parents.

Brad placed his head on a fluffy pillow and closed his eyes. I nestled next to him and sobbed. His tears blended with mine. I drew comfort from the warmth of his body.

An hour passed, and my stomach grumbled. I extracted myself from Brad's arms and stood. Although my appetite had returned, my limbs felt leaden.

Brad sat up. "Hungry?"

"Starving."

While he ordered comfort food for the two of us, which consisted of a couple of juicy cheeseburgers and fries, I texted JP and accepted the earlier offer. Brad had reassured me on the drive over that he meant it when he said it was a good idea.

Tomorrow, we'd meet with Tim's attorney and pick up a copy of his will. When we booked this trip, I never imagined that a law firm would be part of our itinerary.

~ * ~

The morning sun shone through the sliding glass doors leading to our balcony. The heavenly view of the Caribbean was a sharp contrast to the horror of our situation. While I logged into my computer, Brad left for his run.

I called the number that Aaron had provided via email late last night and placed the phone on speaker. As I clicked on the secure link where the files related to the investigation were stored, I sipped my tea. A scanned copy of Tim's manuscript and his research notes had been saved to the drive.

"Thank you, Liz, for joining. Righto. Liz is a PI from the

States. She's helping with the investigation into Tim Knight's death. Since everyone's here, shall we get started?" Aaron introduced the other team members in the room, Sheila, and Felix. His voice boomed over the connection. He explained my role as an investigator familiar with the details of Tim's disappearance. "Our focus today will be the deceased and any possible links to the larger money laundering investigation. We'll begin with the coroner's preliminary report."

I clicked on the file labeled TK Preliminary Postmortem. Aaron explained that the cause of death was unknown, but Tim hadn't drowned. He was dead before he was anchored to the ocean floor. I silently thanked God that he'd not been alive when the sharks had attacked.

He continued, "We'll know more when the toxicology results come back."

The next topic of discussion was forensics. Aaron groaned. "Any evidence from Tim's home has been severely compromised."

I winced. Between the four of us and three pets, I could only imagine.

He pressed on. "A dive team will search the surrounding area where his body was discovered. I'm hopeful that those efforts will produce better results."

I heard the rustle of papers as the commissioner instructed JP to pass out copies of Tim's manuscript and the research notes. And then I caught the sound of an odd scraping noise on the other end of the phone.

"Bloody hell. The rats are back in the ductwork. Sheila, after we finish, tell the receptionist to call the exterminator."

Of course, he assigned that task to the only female in the room.

Aaron continued, "Each of you are to read this after our meeting. The documents are not to leave this room, nor are you to discuss their contents outside of the team. I want a report with your thoughts on any link to our broader investigation by the end of the day. Felix, you'll shred the copies when everyone is done."

An audible grunt sounded from Felix.

"Is there a problem?"

"No, sir. It's just . . . I'm not much of a reader."

"Well, you will be. Shall we carry on? Any questions? Liz? You still with us?"

"Yes, sir. I have no questions." I had plenty of questions, like why was Aaron being so protective over the copies of Tim's story? But I wouldn't be voicing them on the call.

"Liz, you and JP will go to the area where his body was discovered and speak with the couple who found him." Aaron continued to dole out other assignments. "Liz, you are excused. The team needs to discuss the larger case. Do you have anything to add before you drop off?"

"Nope. I'm good." I drummed my fingers on the table. I wasn't used to being dictated to, and I didn't like it. My mentor, Gunner, had always treated me as a partner, not some underling. After the meeting, I placed a call to my former boss.

"Yo, Liz. You back from your honeymoon already?"

"No." I described our current dilemma and the fact that I was temporarily employed by the Royal Cayman Islands Police Service.

After I'd voiced my frustrations about Aaron's leadership style, Gunner said, "Be careful. Remember you're in a foreign territory with its own rules and regulations. Promise me you won't go rogue."

Gunner knew me well. "I promise," I answered, with my fingers crossed behind my back.

~ * ~

After we picked up the copy of Tim's will, we drove to his house. We'd both been shocked to discover that the copyright for Tim's story would transfer to Brad. That meant that Brad stood to inherit any royalties from the story once it was published, and he owned the rights to the book.

Jenny greeted us at the door and enveloped each of us in a hug. The cleaning crew had just finished. The house smelled like lemon and bleach, and I couldn't see a single pet hair.

"What happened to your arms?" She had scratches up and down each forearm.

"Irish. He wasn't too happy about the cat carrier." She rubbed the wounds on her arms. "Poor thing. As soon as I let him out, he darted under the master bed."

Lawson, Snooper, and Duke emerged from the back patio. Duke came barreling toward us. Brad and I both knelt and nestled our faces in his neck. While Snooper pounced on our dog's tail, Duke planted a sloppy kiss on Brad's cheek and then mine.

Minutes later, a rap on Tim's door indicated JP's arrival. I snapped Duke's leash onto his collar and followed JP out to the nondescript sedan. He hadn't protested when I'd asked to bring my dog along, claiming that Duke might be able to sense clues to Tim's demise.

Duke hopped in the backseat, and I opened the driver's side door and then shook my head. I couldn't get used to everything being on the opposite side. Once we were on the road, Duke hung his head out the window, his tongue flopping in the wind.

"So. What's the speculation on cause of death?" I asked.

"There were no visible wounds." He hesitated. "Other than the shark bites. The prevailing theory is that someone poisoned Tim. Of course, given the state of the body, it's difficult to be certain." He turned the air conditioning down a notch. "You comfortable?"

"I'm fine. Go on."

"Our initial hypothesis is that someone killed him in his home and then stuffed him in the trunk of their car. Then after dark, they took a boat out, tied an anchor to his leg, and tossed him in the sea."

I rubbed my chin as I considered the theory. "Plausible." No one had seen Tim since he'd left Becky's apartment, and his luggage and Jeep were at his house. My mind churned as I considered other possibilities.

JP interrupted my thoughts. "Barker's National Park tends to be quieter than the other beaches. The couple who found him were staying at a nearby condominium. We'll speak with them first. Afterward, we'll join the forensics team and conduct our review of the area."

"OK. Any word on the toxicology reports?"

"Aaron's put a rush on it."

"What are your thoughts on the dirty cop in Tim's story?"

"Ma chérie, it is a work of fiction. The laundering details may align with our investigation, but my friend runs a tight ship. I do not believe a corrupt officer would survive under his watch."

"Have you met Dale Foster?"

"Name's familiar. I may have met him on my first day. Why?"

"You might want to check him out."

"Do you believe that he is corrupt?"

"I've heard rumors." I remembered Pearl's comments.

The couple that had discovered Tim's remains met us in the condo's lobby. Avid scuba divers, they were also on the island for their honeymoon. We settled in green vinyl chairs, surrounded by fresh plants. Duke sat next to the young woman, who introduced herself as Sherry. Her hand trembled as she stroked my dog's fur. The man, Ken, recounted the horror of finding the body that had been torn up by sharks. As I flashed back to the image of his corpse in the morgue, I involuntarily shivered.

They'd immediately phoned the police and had considered cutting their trip short. We didn't learn anything new, and Duke didn't yip once. JP handed Ken a card, and we left to connect with the forensic team gathering evidence onshore and offshore.

As we walked the short distance to the beach, JP asked, "When did you get engaged?"

His question surprised me. "Last year."

"Any reason you didn't tell me?"

We'd spoken on the phone at least half a dozen times since then. There really wasn't a good reason to keep it secret. "I don't know. We usually talk about work. I guess it never seemed like the right time."

"D'accord." JP waved at one of the forensic team members combing the beach up ahead. "I like Brad. Perhaps one day I will also be able to call him my friend."

I felt reassured that Duke didn't yip.

Suddenly, Duke jerked his leash and pulled me into a patch of sea grape trees. As he tugged me deeper into the foliage, the large circular leaves brushed my face. He stopped in front of a small motorboat tucked under a shrub. "JP," I shouted. "Over here."

"Where are you?"

"Here." I waved my arms. "Look what Duke found." I wasn't sure if the boat had anything to do with the case, but it warranted examination. "Good boy." I patted my dog's head.

JP joined us. Careful not to touch anything, we peeled back the branches and peered inside. The vessel contained a couple of oars, a bottle of bleach, a can of gasoline, and a torn piece of black fabric.

"You stay here. I will find a member of the team," JP said.

While Duke sat in the shade, I scanned the surroundings and searched for anything suspicious. The ground was indented where the boat had been drug under the tree. Someone had erased any footprints with a palm frond. After several long minutes, JP returned, and we left the experts to do their job.

"I believe Duke earned a steak."

At the word *steak*, my dog lurched toward the car.

We coaxed Duke back to the beach with a treat and conducted a thorough search of the surrounding area. Our efforts produced no additional potential evidence. Then, true to his word, JP treated me to lunch.

Once we'd placed our orders, he described the rigorous reporting requirements to the French and Cayman authorities for the broader money laundering investigation. As a member of the Cayman Anti-Money Laundry Steering Group, the commissioner was required to update various government officials on a regular basis.

"Until we have solid evidence, Aaron is keeping our reports to the various agencies brief."

"Why?" I asked.

The server arrived with our food. After the young man departed, JP responded, "You never know with cases like these who might be involved. Better to err on the side of caution." He cut a few bite-size pieces of his New York strip and placed them on the floor for Duke.

As I savored a shrimp po'boy, I recalled the piece of fabric and the footprint we'd discovered on Mastic Trail yesterday. Since we hadn't found any signs of a struggle, I doubted the location was the scene of the crime, but every clue counted. I disclosed the details to JP and then extracted my notebook from my tote. After I jotted the measurements that I'd taken from the footprint we'd found onto a blank sheet, I tore out the page and handed him the information.

He glanced at the paper and then tucked it into his pocket. "I am surprised you didn't divulge this sooner."

I shrugged. "I didn't think it was relevant. We didn't find anything to indicate that Tim had even been there."

JP interrupted, "We will need to take that fabric and coin into evidence."

"OK. But how about a picture of the coin instead?" I recalled the note on Tim's bed. After all, it was a part of his wedding gift to us.

"D'accord," he exhaled.

My phone pinged with a text from Brad.

I'm finished. Where are you?

Grabbing a bite with JP.

A few seconds passed before I received the next message.

Any progress?

Yeah. Duke found something. I'll fill you in later.

When will you be back?

"JP, are we done for the day?"

"We need to file a report. When can you turn in that piece of fabric and send me the picture?"

I leaned forward and pleaded with my eyes. "How about you take me back to Tim's? I'll give you the swatch and take a photo of the coin. Then when you get back to the station, you can draft the report and send it to me for sign-off."

JP narrowed his eyes. "Liz . . ."

"Please?"

"Alright."

I fingered a short response to Brad.

Soon.

My stomach tightened. Since the 'Duke test,' Brad acted more relaxed around JP, but their interactions had been few. I hoped JP's 'friends' comment wasn't wishful thinking.

Chapter 10

Brad wiped beads of perspiration off his neck. His running shorts and shoes indicated that he'd just come back from his second run of the day. Behind him Lawson struggled to catch his breath. As I admired Brad's toned muscles, I wondered if the call with Tim's brother Jim or my lunch with JP had propelled him to burn off some extra steam. Our dog lunged toward him and begged for a back rub.

"What did Duke find?" Brad massaged our pup's shoulders.

I didn't detect any animosity in Brad's voice, but his jaw was clenched, and his brows were raised.

"JP, why don't you fill him in? I'll get that piece of fabric we found on the trail. Be right back." I exited the room before either one of them could respond.

When I returned, Brad smiled. Lawson was sprawled out on the floor. "Are you OK?" I asked him.

"Man, I could barely keep up with Brad. That dude can run."

As I handed the plastic bag to JP, I breathed a sigh of relief at the lack of tension in the room.

"Brad, do you have the coin? I need to take a picture of it for the investigation."

Brad extracted the gold from his pocket. I snapped a shot of the front and back and handed the piece back to Brad. "Just messaged it to you," I said to JP.

After JP left, Brad said, "Will the evidence from the boat help identify the killer?"

Were we any closer to finding out who murdered Tim? "If it's even connected . . . but it was a good find. Good boy, Duke." He thumped his tail on the floor.

"What's next?"

"As far as I know, I'm done with the investigation for the day. I thought I'd call Becky and ask if she knew a banker with the initials SW. It's weird I haven't heard from her. Have you?"

"Nothing."

"And then why don't we pay Ziggy another visit?"

"With Duke?"

"Of course." I winked.

Jenny entered the room. Snooper trailed behind her. "Hi, Liz. How'd it go?"

"OK . . . We're thinking about going for a boat ride. You two wanna join us?"

"Sounds great." She looked down at Lawson. "Why are you on the floor?"

"Remind me never to go running with Brad again. If you'll help me up, I'm in."

"Poor baby." Before she pulled Lawson upright, Jenny bent down and kissed his cheek.

While Brad changed, I placed a call to Becky. She picked up on the first ring, and I heard sniffles in the background. Since it was Saturday, she was likely either at home or the shelter.

"Did you hear the news about Tim? I can't believe he's gone," she wailed.

"Yes, we did. It's terrible."

The tone of Becky's voice became indignant. "When did *you* find out?"

"Yesterday."

"And you're just now calling me?" she sputtered and then blew her nose.

Well, she could have phoned us. "I'm sorry."

"It's OK . . . I guess." She hesitated. "I feel awful that the last time I saw Tim we fought."

"Where are you?" I asked.

"Home. My face is so puffy. I can't go out in public."

I rolled my eyes.

Becky continued, "It's awful. A cop came by last night. I know I could've called you too, but I can't stop crying."

"I can't imagine how difficult this is for you."

"That guy asked me a bunch of questions. Like I was a suspect or something." She hiccupped.

"They're just doing their job."

"I guess so," she muttered.

I changed the subject. "Becky, Tim had a note on his calendar for a visit with a banker with the initials SW. Do you know who that is?"

"Spencer Webb. I set that up. Tim needed to interview someone in the finance industry for research. He's a longtime family friend and my boss. Why do you ask?"

"Just curious. Is there anything I can do for you?"

"Not right now. I'll call you later, OK?"

After she ended the call, I noted that she hadn't bothered to ask how we fared.

~   *   ~

On the drive to Ziggy's Tours and Charters, the four of us agreed on a loose approach to sleuth out information from Ziggy. Once we were on the boat, we'd chat about Tim's exciting new thriller. I'd casually ask Ziggy if he knew Tim once again. Based on his response, we'd wing any further questions. I explained to Jenny and Lawson that I'd studied body language and voice inflection. I'd sense if Ziggy lied. Of course, I also had Duke. If he yipped, I'd know the man was lying.

Snooper wasn't happy when we left him behind, but we'd all agreed that the puppy was too young for a boat ride.

By the time we pulled into the parking lot, it was late afternoon. I hoped Ziggy was still around. Brad brought plenty of cash to entice him to take us for a ride. Before I could put the leash on Duke, he jumped out of the car and dashed past a woman walking into the store.

After I caught up with our dog, I was relieved to see Ziggy behind the counter. As I struggled to catch my breath, I managed to gasp, "I'm sorry."

"Can't cha' read da sign? Dey be no pooches allowed in here. He don't bite do he?"

I snapped the leash to Duke's collar. "No. He's friendly." Our dog's nose wiggled as he sniffed the smells of saltwater, sweat, and a variety of snacks.

Brad sauntered inside, followed by Jenny and Lawson.

"I recognize youse." Ziggy pointed at Brad and me. "You da newlyweds. What can I do for ya?" He grinned. "Jes got me some new t-shirts." Ziggy held up a teal-colored tee with 'If it Zigs, it Zags' written across the front in flowing black cursive.

"That's us," I replied. "We'd like to take another tour with our friends and our dog. No snorkeling. Just a boat ride."

"I'm about to close. And I don't take no dogs."

Brad pulled out his wallet and extracted ten one hundred dollar bills. "How much for the tour and four of those t-shirts?"

Ziggy rubbed his chin as he studied the cash. "With da dog?"

Brad nodded.

"Fifteen hundra fifty."

Brad pulled out six more hundreds. "Keep the change."

"No, no. Ziggy charge fair prices." He handed Brad five tens.

Ziggy tossed Brad four t-shirts and then locked up the shop.

We strolled to the dock and climbed on the boat. Brad insisted that Duke wear a life jacket. Since his sister's accident, he was vigilant about water safety. Ziggy handed each of us a beer, popped one for himself, and motored out to the Caribbean. He hummed a tune that sounded vaguely like "Rock the Boat" by The Hues Corporation.

As the shoreline faded, I said, "I can't wait for Tim's book to come out."

"It sounds like a real page turner. Secrets . . . money laundering . . . murder." Jenny rubbed her hands together.

Ziggy choked on his beer.

"Yeah, it's a great read. I bet it'll be a best seller," Brad added.

"What book you be talking bout?" Ziggy asked.

"Our friend Tim Knight's book. We told you he'd gone missing on our last tour. Are you a reader?" I asked.

"Yep, but don't member dat name. You find him?"

Duke yipped. Was the yip related to the reader comment or his knowledge of Tim? Maybe both.

Brad answered, "Not yet." That earned another yip from our dog. Tim had been found . . . dead.

"Are you sure you never met him?" I asked. "He mentioned you once."

"Nevah met da man. Meybe different Ziggy?" Duke yipped again. "What's da matter with your pooch?"

Brad rubbed our dog's ears. "Probably just nervous. It's his first boat ride." Duke emitted a half-bark, half-whine.

"Well shut him da hell up." He revved the engine and sped out into the turquoise sea.

When Ziggy pulled the throttle back, I asked, "Have you heard any rumors about buried treasure on the island?"

Brad shot me a look. We hadn't discussed this line of questioning.

"Dey be plenty of treasure on da island." He expounded on sunken ships and discovered bounty.

"What about onshore?" I asked.

"Dey be rumors. None of dem true. Trust me, if dere be treasure, Ziggy find it."

No yip from Duke.

~ * ~

After the tour, we piled back into the Jeep. In the back, Duke hung his head out the vehicle, and Jenny scratched our dog's head. "What do you think, Liz? Was the guy lying?"

I turned toward the back seat as Brad put the car in reverse. "He definitely knew Tim."

"I agree. The way he gripped the steering wheel and the tone of his voice . . ."

"You might have a future as a PI," I teased.

"No. I'd totally want to be an amateur. Just like Velma."

Lawson shrugged. "He might be lying but that doesn't mean the guy murdered him. How do we figure out if he did?"

I cringed at the *we* comment. What if I'd put the two of them in danger? I scolded myself for not thinking through this earlier. "If he's mixed up in the laundering, he has motive. And if he believes we've read Tim's story, he'll be rattled. His next moves will be telling."

"How can we help?" Lawson asked.

I hesitated and then said, "Can you run some checks on a cop named Dale Foster? Family, bank balances, credit card debt, whatever you can find." Better to keep Jenny and Lawson behind the scenes from now on.

"Sure. I'll start as soon as we get back to the house."

"Any luck finding Tim's phone records?" I asked.

"I'm not as familiar with the systems for the providers here, but there's only a couple. I'll figure it out."

I had no doubt that he would.

"You going to share all of this with Aaron and JP?" Brad asked.

"Of course," I answered.

Duke yipped.

Brad frowned.

Jenny asked, "What's going to happen to Tim's pets?"

"I'm not sure," Brad said. "Tim's sister-in-law is allergic, so his brother can't take them."

Jenny thought for a moment. "Can I adopt them? Snooper's so cute, and I can't imagine separating him from Irish."

Lawson's eyes narrowed. "You know I don't like cats."

"So? It's not like we're living together or anything."

Jenny's jaw was set. "The poor babies need a home."

As he stared out the window, Lawson mumbled, "Whatever."

"There were no stipulations in his will about the pets. I don't see any reason why you can't take them," Brad replied.

Jenny clapped, and a wide grin spread across her face. "Awesome."

Once we'd dropped Jenny, Lawson, and Duke off at Tim's, we returned to our hotel. Lawson hadn't said another word the entire trip. I prayed that they'd mend the earlier tiff.

Brad grabbed my hands and whispered in my ear, "Care to step into a rainforest?" He planted tender kisses along my neck.

I followed him into the bathroom. While he turned the handles of the dual showerheads, I shed my clothes and joined him. The pulsating stream of water and the steamy lovemaking was pure bliss.

After we toweled off, we slipped into the plush hotel-provided terry cloth robes. Brad ordered room service and then poured each of us a generous glass of white wine. While we sat on the balcony, we watched the sun cast hues of lavender, apricot, and gray as it made its descent on the horizon.

"You're going to tell JP and Aaron about our boat ride with Ziggy and that the SW stands for Spencer Webb, right?"

I took a large gulp of pinot grigio. "Um, not yet."

"Why not?" Brad narrowed his eyes. So much for the earlier honeymoon bliss.

"I need to find out more about Dale Foster, the alleged dirty cop, and his relationship with Aaron. What if the commissioner is somehow involved? Everyone on this island seems connected."

"Why wouldn't you relay the information to JP, even if he is friends with Aaron? You trust him, don't you?"

"Yes."

"Well, JP's the one who said we're all in danger. He needs to know what we've learned. What if we set Ziggy off today?"

"I have a gun." I grinned.

"Not funny."

Gunner's words replayed in my mind. Brad was right. I needed to divulge what I knew to JP. "OK. I promise. As soon as I can, I'll update him."

"Call him now."

"I'd rather tell him in person."

"Fine," he replied just as our food arrived. I stood to follow Brad back inside and caught another glint of light from the same hotel room as before. A second later, I heard a whizzing sound, and then something slammed into the wrought iron railing and fragmented into pieces.

A bullet.

I dodged back into our room and slid the door shut.

After Brad placed the tray of food on the round glass-top dining table, he glanced up at my face and asked, "Is something wrong?"

I held up a finger. "I'll tell you in in minute." I closed the drapes and phoned JP.

Once I'd recounted our near miss on the balcony, he said, "We will send someone over right away."

Brad dropped the steel cover he'd just removed from the plate. "Somebody shot at us?"

I nodded and then resumed my conversation with JP. "I don't want Aaron to know about any of this."

Brad folded his arms and glared at me. I turned my back. His body language was a distraction.

"Mon Dieu. Why?"

"Not yet. Not until after I find out more about Dale Foster and any connections he might have to the commissioner."

"C'est ridicule. I have known Aaron for years. He would never be involved with something unlawful."

Since he'd started answering in his native tongue, I could tell JP was agitated, but I needed for him to wait before talking to his friend. "Just give me a little more time, OK?"

"So, you can be assassiné? Non."

"If someone wanted to kill me, they would've. It was just a warning shot."

Several seconds of silence followed before JP responded, "Merde . . . I will be by in the morning at six sharp to pick up the evidence. If you discover anything or if anything else happens, you are to inform me immediately. You have until after tomorrow's call. After that, I will share everything with Aaron. In the meantime, stay safe inside."

"We have a call on Sunday?"

"Liz." JP groaned.

"OK. I'll see you tomorrow morning."

"This so-called plan of yours is garbage," Brad said after I hung up the phone. "Do you want to get us killed?"

"No," I grumbled. "I'm trying to find out who murdered Tim. Can you just trust me on this?"

Brad answered with a sigh.

Before I ate my lukewarm meal, I texted Lawson.

Can you put a rush on the information I asked for?

He responded immediately.

On it.

After we'd finished our dinner in uncomfortable silence, Lawson called. Not only was Dale Foster up to his ears in debt, but he was also Aaron's first cousin. Their mothers were sisters. I fought to keep the 'told you so' out of my voice when I updated JP and Brad.

Chapter 11

The next morning, I woke up at five forty-five, threw on some clothes, and brewed a pot of fresh coffee. True to his word, JP rapped at our door at six. Brad was in the shower. The sweet floral and nutty aroma of the local brew permeated the room.

I poured each of us a cup, and we stepped onto the balcony. JP set his steaming mug on a table, slipped on gloves, and then used a pair of tweezers to extract the fragments. After he placed the evidence in a bag, he said, "To be safe, we should go back inside." He grabbed his coffee and led the way.

After I slid the sliding glass door shut, JP asked, "Which direction did it come from?"

I pointed at the opposing condominiums.

"And that is the same spot where someone spied on you before?"

I nodded. "I'm not one hundred percent certain, but I believe so."

"And when did that occur?"

So much had happened. I counted the days off in my head. "Um. Three maybe four days ago."

While JP sipped his coffee, he estimated the location of the room. "Seven stories up. Three from the end. D'accord. I will speak with the manager. Perhaps I can find the culprit."

"I'll go with you. Let me put on some shoes."

Brad entered the room. "Good morning." He gestured toward the evidence bag on the table. "Is that what's left of the bullet?"

"Yes. I was about to explain to your wife that accompanying me to question the manager of the condominiums across the way is a bad idea."

Brad shook his head. "Liz, why would you do that?"

I crossed my arms and addressed JP. "Why not?"

"Because either someone broke into that condo, or the culprit had a key."

"So, what?" I said.

"That means the list of suspects could include the manager or an employee. If someone spots you, they may bolt."

He had a point. "Fine. You'll update me on what you find?"

"Thank God," Brad muttered under his breath.

"Of course." JP took one last sip of joe before he headed out the door.

Half an hour later, JP phoned. He said that the manager claimed that the condo was vacant on the dates in question. When JP flashed his badge, the man divulged the name of the company that owned the unit, Capital Management LLC. He then escorted him to the seventh floor and allowed him to search the space. The condo appeared to have been recently cleaned, and JP found no signs of a weapon or binoculars.

Since I had time before this morning's call, I got ready for the day. JP texted me shortly before our meeting.

Spoke with Aaron about last night's incident.

I thought he was going to wait until after the call, but whatever.

And?

He wanted to take you off the case. I reminded him that one of the reasons we brought you on board was to keep you safe. So, he agreed to keep you on. For the moment.

Thanks. I think.

He will put a rush on the ballistics, and I will investigate the owner of the unit. Please do not do anything . . . how do you say? Do not go rogue.

Dang. I was beginning to develop a reputation.

After I joined the call, Aaron kicked off the meeting. He didn't waste time with pleasantries. "We received the toxicology report. Liz, it's located in the shared folder. JP, please pass out the copies."

As I clicked on the document, I heard a rustle of papers on the other end of the phone.

Aaron continued, "Large amounts of pentobarbital were discovered in the body. It's determined to be the cause of death. The drug is a barbiturate typically used as a sedative. Although in large quantities, it can be deadly."

I examined the report. "How was it administered?"

Aaron cleared his throat. "Based on the analysis, most likely injected. We didn't find any traces in his stomach."

Felix asked, "Any idea of the source?"

Aaron answered, "Not yet. Sheila, I want you to research all possible legal and illegal channels of obtaining the drug. I expect a list by this afternoon."

"This afternoon?"

"Is that a problem?"

"Um, no, sir."

"Felix, did you destroy all copies of the manuscript and notes?" Aaron asked.

"Yes, sir. I shredded them as instructed."

"Well done."

I searched the file folder for a digital copy of either the manuscript or Tim's notes and came up empty. "What happened to the scanned copy of Tim's story and research notes on the drive? I can't seem to find them."

Clicks on keyboards carried through the line. Even though I wasn't in the room, I could sense the unease. The silence that followed spanned several long seconds.

"Merde," JP exclaimed. "They are gone."

"Impossible." Aaron's voice rose a few notches. "Felix, you're excused. Get with IT and find those files. Pronto." He released a heavy breath. "I'm sure the files were backed-up. Shall we carry on?" Without waiting for a response, Aaron said, "Righto. I've reviewed everyone's reports on the manuscript and compiled a list of potential connections to the overarching investigation." Another crackling of paper resounded in the background. "Liz, I didn't receive a report from you."

"Sorry. I didn't realize that I was supposed to submit one." I opened the file titled 'Connections' and scanned the document.

"Well, then, could you please divulge your initial assessment to the team?"

My mind whirled. Since I wanted to gauge his reaction, I said, "I think the dirty cop in the story could be Dale Foster."

There was an audible gasp in the room, and I wished that I could see everyone's face.

"What makes you believe Dale is dirty?" Aaron spat the last word out.

"I did some research. He has a lot of debt."

"That's hardly damning. Did you also know that he's my first cousin? I highly doubt he's selling information behind my back." Aaron hesitated. I thought he was about to dismiss the idea, but then he said, "JP, see what you can find out and be discreet. This conversation does not leave this room. Understood? And Liz, after this call, you and I will have a talk about your source who divulged my cousin's financial problems."

How was I going to wiggle out of that one?

"Anything else, Liz?"

I shared my misgivings about Ziggy.

Aaron said, "I put Ziggy on the list. His name came up several times as part of the broader investigation surrounding the money laundering. Any other comments?"

"What about the boat we found?" I asked.

"I've put a rush on the forensics report, but it's the weekend. I should have something by tomorrow morning." He cleared his throat and continued, "When Felix returns, I'll ask him to search the designated area in Mastic Trail to assess if we should allocate more resources to follow that lead. Liz, I expect you to provide him with directions."

"OK."

Before he ended the meeting, the commissioner divided up individuals for research, surveillance, and questioning.

Lucky me. JP and I got the group of bankers. Since the banks were closed on Sunday, I had the day off, or so I thought.

~   *   ~

After Aaron ended the call, he phoned and insisted I meet him in a city called Hell, a popular tourist spot. He claimed the location would be out of range of listening ears. Originally, the place had been on my list of sites to visit. Now it felt like confirmation of our situation.

As a favor to Tim's brother, Brad had agreed to meet with the mortuary to get general information about arrangements and costs. Tim had left a note with his will that contained instructions on the type of service he preferred. Since we could only tell a select few about his death, and we had no idea when the body would be released, the specifics would have to be finalized later. Brad would drop me off in Hell on the way to his appointment with the funeral home.

As he drove, I kept my eyes glued to the side mirror and

checked for a tail. If we had one, they were experienced enough to avoid detection. Brad glanced a few times in the rearview mirror. Neither one of us voiced our fears, but the emotion simmered in the air.

Instead, I shared the disappearance of Tim's thriller from the station's server. My voice rose in concern. "What if they lost all of his work?"

"Liz, relax. When Tim copyrighted the story, he had to attach a copy. The manuscript is preserved for at least the next fifty years."

I recalled that a copy of Tim's research notes existed on the Cloud and released a sigh of relief.

"Strange that he did that so soon. I thought that happened right before you published," Brad added.

"Maybe he didn't want anyone to steal the story."

Brad pulled into Hell's parking lot. "You're probably right," he said before he kissed me goodbye.

After he drove off, I explored the grounds while I waited for Aaron. Since it was early, the crowd was sparse. A painted mural of a devil provided an idyllic spot for tourists to snap a picture and commemorate their visit to Hell. I spotted a gift shop. After the meeting with Aaron, I'd pop in and buy postcards to send to my parents and my neighbor Lou.

As I walked the wooden walkway that bordered black pinnacles of limestone, I paused and read the sign with the history of Hell. There were various theories about how the place earned the name. The prevailing belief involved an early British Commissioner who joked that the twenty-four-million-year-old limestone formations resembled Hell itself, and the name stuck. As I continued to read, I sensed someone watching me and shivered despite the heat.

While I studied the geological formation the size of half a football field, I scanned the surrounding area for any hints of danger. I jumped when I felt a tap on my shoulder.

"Didn't mean to spook you. Shall we take a seat?" Aaron motioned toward the benches by the store.

"Sure." As we progressed toward a bench, I tried to shake off the earlier vibes of being watched. "Sorry to be so jumpy. I got a creepy feeling that somebody was following me." I glanced over my shoulder for any signs of a tail.

"This place will do that to you."

"Yeah. I guess so."

"I understand that you've experienced some threats, including being shot at, and I have no problem if you'd like to back out."

"Um, that would be a no." *A Hell no.* "Any luck finding those missing files?"

"I'm confident IT will have a back-up."

I didn't tell him about the copyrighted copy or the saved copy of the notes. My intuition nudged me to hold back.

As I settled next to Aaron, I dreaded the lecture I expected to receive about my research into his cousin.

Instead, he said, "Liz, you are a valued member of my team. JP has an immense amount of respect for you, and I do too. I'm glad that you've decided to continue on. Both you and JP need to be my outside ears, and I must be able to trust you. Explicitly."

"OK . . ." I waited for him to elaborate.

"I have my own misgivings about Dale, but I couldn't voice them in front of the team. He's always been a bit of a troublemaker. Even when we were kids. I hired him on to the force as a favor to my aunt." He gazed at his hands. "I suppose I shouldn't be surprised he might be crooked. But it stings. I want you and JP to help me find out if the information contained in Tim's manuscript is true."

"Your aunt lives on the island?"

"Yes. She's my mum's sister. They're very close."

"And your mother lives here, too?"

Aaron explained that his parents and his only sibling, a sister, lived just outside of Windsor, England. His mom was a solicitor, and his dad taught physics at Windsor College.

"What if the speculation about Dale is real?"

"I'll deal with it." Aaron's shoulders slumped. "Right now, we are keeping the details of the money laundering investigation close to the vest. I appreciate it if you'd do the same."

I wished that Duke was here with me. Although JP trusted Aaron, I wasn't quite there yet. "You said you wanted to know my source?"

"Oh. That was just bluster. No need."

"I don't mind." I shared Lawson's name and praised his computer capabilities.

"Thank you, Liz. I'd like for you and JP to keep tabs on Dale today."

Damn. Another day in paradise . . . shot.

Aaron stood. "JP will be here at ten, and then you two can get to work. I'm going to follow up with Tim's girlfriend." He grinned.

I imagined that he was looking forward to a conversation with the island's former beauty pageant queen. "You don't think Becky did it, do you?"

"Doesn't have an alibi, but I doubt it. She's an attractive woman." He tapped his head and then winked. "But not too much up here."

"What do you mean she doesn't have an alibi? She said she was at work the day Tim went missing."

"Said she never went in. Claims she was too upset after her argument with Tim." He cleared his throat. "Righto, then. I'll be off. I expect a report back from you and JP."

Righto, Aaron.

After he left, I texted Lawson.

Find out everything you can about Aaron Holmes and his family. He's originally from Windsor, England. His mom's a solicitor there, and his dad works for Windsor College.

I received an immediate reply.

On it.

The aunt, too.

You got it.

A glance at my phone confirmed that I had fifteen minutes to shop. I sent a quick text to Brad.

No need to pick me up. Looks like I'm working today.

OK. Everything good with the Commish?

Yeah. I'll check in with you later.

Brad sent me a thumbs up.

~　*　~

JP parked across the street a block down from Dale's home. The white van's dark-tinted windows made it impossible for a passerby to see the two of us inside. Dale's peach stucco home was one of the smaller houses in the area, yet still lovely with a well-manicured lawn and lush landscaping.

"Pretty nice neighborhood for a cop's salary," I commented.

"Dale bought the house two years ago for over half a million. He has two kids in private school, and his wife is a stay-at-home mother," JP said.

"That's one way to rack up the debt." The street was quiet. No kids playing in the front yards. No one walking their dog. I made small talk to fill the silence. "What's new with you? Any girlfriends?"

"One prospect. But she just wanted to be friends. Then she got married."

Gulp. Blood rushed to my face, and I adjusted the passenger side air conditioning down a notch. Thankfully, the awkward moment was interrupted when a garage door raised, and a black Jaguar sedan backed out of Dale's driveway. JP turned on the ignition and prepared to follow.

We tailed Dale into Georgetown. Although nothing else had happened since the bullet scare, I kept my eyes on the sideview mirror. After Dale pulled his car into the last space in a tiny lot adjacent to a waterfront restaurant, JP drove into the public parking garage across the street. He turned off the ignition, fetched a bag from behind the seat, and tossed me a Cayman Islands shirt, matching cap, and a pair of sunglasses.

"You want me to change? Here?"

"Hurry. We don't want to lose him."

"Look the other way."

Ever the gentleman, he turned toward the door and donned his own tourist disguise, complete with a fanny pack. I held back a giggle. JP with a belly bag was quite the sight.

We hustled out of the van and across the road to the restaurant.

"We're meeting a friend of ours." I described Dale to the hostess.

"The cop?"

I nodded.

"He's at his usual spot at the bar on the patio." She handed us two menus and pointed in the direction of the outdoor deck.

JP and I located a table away from the crowd and next to the water. We had a decent view of Dale at the bar. While he sipped on a Caybrew, Dale chatted with the bartender. We weren't close enough to catch any of the conversation.

Two young women giggled as they stepped out onto the deck. One of them wore a short, peach, spaghetti-strap sundress. She carried a large duffle bag that didn't match her outfit. The other had on an aqua skorts jumpsuit and a floppy straw hat. They both wore oversized sunglasses. Peachy took a seat on the barstool next to Dale and flipped her long blonde hair over her shoulder. Aqua sat next to her. They said something to the bartender, and then Peachy leaned down and set the duffle bag on the wooden floor.

While the scene unfolded, the server arrived with our beers and a basket of conch fritters. JP closed out the check.

The bartender returned and set two large frozen daiquiris in front of the women. They sipped their drinks, ignoring Dale. Twenty minutes later, the two departed leaving the duffle bag behind. Dale paid out his tab and picked up the bag.

My heart raced as we bustled out of the restaurant. Over our drinks, we'd agreed that if needed, we'd split up. JP would follow Dale, and I'd tail the girls and attempt to find out their names and where they were from.

"You have the weapon Aaron gave you?" JP asked.

I patted my shoulder bag.

"Be careful, ma chérie." He gave me a peck on the cheek.

I waited outside as the pair disappeared inside a boutique clothing store. After half an hour, they stepped out. Both carried a bag with the shop's logo. The next stop was a souvenir store. Perspiration dribbled down my back, and I followed them inside to get a break from the heat.

I approached the section of the store where Peachy and Aqua shopped for souvenirs. The two of them stopped by a fake spruce in the corner. I joined them and studied the array of Cayman-themed Christmas ornaments on the branches.

"Lisa, what about this one?"

Aqua picked up a porcelain Santa dressed in swim trunks.

"No way. It says Grand Cayman on it. How 'bout this one?" Lisa pointed at a globe painted with a beach framed by palm trees.

"You're right. That one's much better." Peachy plucked it from the branch.

"Where are you two from?" I asked.

"Denver. You?" Peachy said.

"South Carolina." Maybe I should buy a memento, too. I fingered a clear glass ball with colored sand. "Name's Liz Adams. Oops. I mean O'Connor. I just got married. I'm here on my honeymoon."

"I'm Lisa, um, Smith. This is my friend Tara Jones," Aqua said. Tara poked Lisa in the ribs.

I wondered if those were their real names. A glass sand dollar shaped ornament caught my eye. I picked it off the tree and eyed the price. "Where are you staying?" I asked.

"The Sandbox Condominiums," Lisa replied. "A friend of ours is letting us use it for free."

"C'mon. We need to go work on our tans." Tara nudged her friend toward the front of the store.

As the pair turned to head for the cash register, I said, "Enjoy the rest of your vacation." Interesting. I recalled that the Sandbox Condominiums were directly across from our hotel. The same building the bullet came from.

I trailed behind them, hoping to catch a glimpse of a credit card with one of their names. No such luck. They both paid cash.

After I made my purchase, I stepped outside and checked in with JP. He reported that Dale had stopped at Ziggy's Tours and Charters and disappeared inside with the duffle bag. He was camped in the van waiting for Dale to return. I mentioned that the girls were staying at the Sandbox Condominiums.

A few seconds passed as JP mulled over the lead. "Perhaps coincidence, perhaps not. I will look into it. Can you entertain yourself? It will likely be a little while before I can pick you up."

"No worries. I'll call Brad."

"I just spotted Dale, and he doesn't have the bag. I will call you later." After a hasty goodbye, JP ended the call.

I wondered what was in the duffle . . . drugs, cash, or something else? And how did Ziggy's place fit in? Maybe I shouldn't quit yet. Might be worth finding the girls to see if they'd divulge any further details about their trip and the duffle bag they left behind.

I phoned Brad. As I waited for his arrival, I started the hunt.

Chapter 12

After a fruitless search through the streets of Georgetown, Brad and I called it quits. Maybe I'd meander over to the condominium complex later and attempt to find the young women. Since we'd barely spent any time on the beach, we fetched our swimsuits from the hotel and headed to Tim's house. Hours spent listening to waves with our dog beside us sounded divine.

Jenny chose to lounge by the pool, while Lawson attempted to hack the phone providers and research Aaron's history. Brad and I hauled chairs, a cooler, a bag full of snacks, an umbrella, and towels down to the stretch of sand behind Tim's home.

Brad's brows furrowed and a pained expression crossed his face.

As I rubbed suntan lotion onto my skin, I said, "What's on your mind?"

"I was thinking about the day we closed the deal on Multipoint Protection Services."

I nodded, encouraging him to continue the story of the sale of his identity theft protection company.

"Tim and I went straight to our favorite Irish bar to celebrate. After we'd toasted and downed the first glass of McCallan, I realized that we'd no longer be working side by side. We vowed to keep in contact. I lost count of how many drinks I had that night." He shook his head. "At least it was the good stuff."

Before I settled in my seat, I kissed his cheek. "I'm sorry. This whole thing sucks."

"Yeah. I can't believe he's gone."

Snooper and Duke provided some comic relief as they chased chickens along the shore. Duke snuck up on a rooster, and it froze. Snooper caught up, bowed down, and then yapped at the bird. The rooster hollered a cocka-doodle-doo back. A flock of chickens turned the tables and began to chase the dogs. Once the pups had exhausted themselves, they curled under the umbrella for a snooze. The chickens waddled away with relief that the chase was over.

I closed my eyes and lifted my face toward the warm sun. Emotions overwhelmed me, and tears pricked at the back of my eyes. I stood. "I'm going for a walk." At the word 'walk,' Duke awoke from his deep slumber.

"Need company?" Brad stretched his legs and wiggled his toes in the sand.

"No, you relax. I'd rather go alone." Sorrow tugged at my soul. At the same time, the details of the investigation whirled in my mind. Maybe a stroll along the beach would help me sort out my emotions and thoughts. I pulled Duke's leash out of my tote and clipped it to his collar. Snooper was sound asleep. "Be back in a bit." I kissed the top of Brad's head. He smelled like Coppertone.

When I turned my back, rivers of tears flowed down my cheeks. My heart squeezed. I missed Tim, too. When I'd worked the identity theft case in Carmel, we'd become friends. I'd envisioned decades of a shared friendship with Brad and me. And to top it off, my honeymoon was a disaster. Ruined. Wrecked. Yes, I was having an all-out, well-deserved pity party.

Duke whined.

"It's OK, boy." I patted his head. Once I was out of Brad's sight, I took off my sunglasses and wiped my wet face with my cover-up.

I jumped when someone came up to my side and poked my arm.

The man spoke in a low, harsh voice. "You need to chill, mon. Stay away from da police and quit poking your nose where it don't belong. Dis island has eyes. Back off and nothing bad happen."

I caught the side of his profile partially hidden by a gray hoodie. My dog emitted a low growl, and the man dashed off before I could get a good look at the rest of his face. I studied his back and etched the image in my memory. Duke tugged on the leash. I considered rushing back to tell Brad what had happened and then dismissed the idea. He had enough on his mind. I was a big girl, and there was no imminent danger. I could handle this.

As I drew in a few deep breaths, I wondered if the warning was related to the bullet shot. Had Aaron received the ballistic report? With everything that had happened, I'd forgotten to ask. I fingered a quick text to Aaron and was surprised when I received an immediate reply.

The bullet was common. The evidence didn't provide any clues to identify the culprit.

OK. Thanks.

As I processed his response, the sound of the waves soothed my rattled emotions. A pair of kayakers navigated the waters ahead. I eyed a blue-and-white fishing boat anchored in the distance. While I admired the homes along the shore, my mind returned to the case. When Duke stopped and sniffed a piece of driftwood, I texted JP.

Now a good time to talk?

My phone rang within seconds.

"I heard the ballistics evidence was a dead end."

"Oui."

"What else happened with Dale?" I asked.

"Nil. After he dropped the bag off, he went home."
"Except . . ." he hesitated.

"What?"

"He may have spotted me. He did not take the same route to his house. I was under the impression he was headed elsewhere and changed his mind."

"Any idea what was in the bag?"

"Most likely cash. Dale had a manilla envelope in his hand when he left. C'est possible that Ziggy launders the money through the tours, and Dale gets a cut. This may be a break in the broader investigation."

I remembered the sign next to the shop's door offering

discounts for cash and the flyer on the counter advertising other tourist businesses that offered the same deal. Was the change that Brad received dirty? "Have you shared this with Aaron?"

"Yes."

"And . . ."

"He promised he would not confront Dale without consulting with me first."

I shared my earlier encounter on the beach.

"Mon Dieu. This is becoming more dangerous. I wonder if it is connected to the other incidents."

"Maybe. If so, it was just another warning. We must be getting closer."

Silence followed. "JP, you still there?"

"Oui," he sighed. "I regret that we involved you."

"I don't." I turned and headed back to Tim's place with a renewed resolve. "We're going to solve this." I picked up the pace. "The bad guys aren't going to win."

"D'accord. Tomorrow we visit the bankers." The tone of his voice was filled with resignation. "I will pick you up after our meeting."

"I have a better idea. Pick me up before. I'll attend in person." I wanted to see faces.

As I approached the house, Lawson ran down to the beach.

"I got it!" He waved a handful of printouts in the air. "Phone records for the last month. And Tim's contacts."

"Great job. What did you find out about Aaron and his family?"

Lawson tugged on his goatee. "Everything checked out. His mom is a big deal solicitor in Windsor. Dad works for the local college. His entire family is clean. Not even a traffic ticket. The aunt is another story. Her husband had a heart attack ten years ago. Didn't leave her with much of anything. She works at a grocery store on the island."

I unhooked Duke from his leash, and he and Snooper resumed their chicken chase. "What about Aaron?"

"Nothing." Lawson handed me the printouts.

I sat in the chair and shielded the documents from spying eyes. Although no one else was on the stretch of beach behind Tim's house, someone could be peering through binoculars from a distance.

After I perused Tim's list of contacts, I searched for Becky's number in the records. On the day of his disappearance, she'd tried to reach him fifteen times. As I continued to study the names and phone numbers, I found one with the initial J. First name Jax. No last name. I racked my brain to recall the name of the bar written on Tim's calendar on the date he met with J. As I ran through the alphabet in my head, I landed on L. Lizard Lounge.

"Anything interesting?" Brad asked.

"Yeah." I pulled my phone out of my beach bag and googled the address. "In the mood for an early cocktail?"

"Sure. I'll go change."

"No need to dress up. This place isn't fancy."

"Want company?" Jenny asked.

"Do you mind staying with the pets? I think it's best if it's just the two of us."

"Not at all." From the pout on her face, I could tell she was disappointed.

While Brad and I walked to the bar, I shared my earlier encounter on the beach.

"I don't like it. This is getting dangerous."

Almost JP's exact sentiment. "It means we're getting close."

"I don't want you going anywhere by yourself."

"OK." I was glad Duke wasn't around since he would've yipped at my response. As we strolled hand in hand, we were silent, both of us lost in thought. Whenever we passed by bushes, my pulse quickened, and my senses went on high alert. I half expected someone to jump out. When we arrived safely at our destination, I drew in a deep breath of relief.

Despite the 'no smoking' signs, the smell of cigarettes hung in the air of the dark, dank bar. The stench likely came from the patrons' clothes and hair. This was not a place tourists frequented. More likely it was a spot where drug deals were negotiated, and secret lovers met.

We found two open barstools at the long black bar top. The woman behind the counter wore a black t-shirt with a lizard emblazoned across the front. "Haven't seen you two in here before. What can I get you?" She set a couple of cardboard coasters in front of us.

I imagined she was younger than she looked. She had the appearance of a smoker who spent a lot of time in the sun. "I'll take a glass of your house chardonnay."

She smirked at me and then winked at Brad.

"And you, handsome?"

"A glass of your best scotch on ice with a splash of water."

"You got it."

Brad handed her his credit card. "And a drink for you. Whatever you want." He winked.

I leaned back in my chair. She was much more likely to respond to Brad than to me, so I let him take the lead. After she set down our drinks, she cozied up to Brad from the other side of the bar with a rum and Coke and introduced herself. "I'm Lexie." She batted her eyelashes.

I wiped leftover lipstick off my glass with a napkin. Yuck.

Brad responded. "Brad and Liz. We're visiting the island. Our friend Tim Knight lives here. He recommended this place."

"Tim?"

"You know him?"

"Yeah, he's a regular. Haven't seen him in about a week. Last time he was here was with Jax." Her smile dropped, and she made a sign of the cross. "May he rest in peace."

I was baffled. Was the word out? "Tim?" I asked.

"No, darling, Jax. It's tragic." She drew the syllables of darling out as she leaned forward and explained in a conspiratorial tone. "He was murdered." She drew her finger across her neck. "Someone slit his throat and dumped him in an alley. Rumor has it that he was a snitch and double-crossed the wrong person. Funeral's tomorrow. This place will be packed after the service."

Was Jax the informant that was killed? I shot off a quick text to JP.

Brad leaned over to see who I was texting and then asked, "Did Tim meet anyone else up here?"

"Occasionally his girlfriend Becky joined him. That girl is something else. I don't know what Tim sees in her."

Even though I one hundred percent agreed, I asked, "Why do you say that?"

"Jealous. Controlling. Need I say more? Tim deserves way better."

At least she referred to Tim in the present tense. My phone pinged with a response from JP with the full name of the informant. I showed the response to Brad. "Is Jax the same as Jackson Jeffries?"

"Yes. That's his full name, but everyone calls him Jax." Lexie sighed. "So sad. He was only thirty-eight. He worked for his father's boat charter business. Jax was the most requested charter guide." Lexie shook her head. "His parents must be devastated."

"Where's the service?" Brad asked.

Lexie shared the details, and I jotted them on a cocktail napkin. I was beginning to feel like I was in the sequel to the movie *Four Weddings and a Funeral*. Only this one was titled, *Two Funerals and a Honeymoon*.

~ * ~

The main conference room at the police station needed a new paint job. The whiteboard was littered with specks of leftover marker, and the scent of stale coffee hung in the air. Before the meeting started, I introduced myself to Felix and Sheila. Felix was

Black with a shaved head. He looked like he should be on a basketball court. On the other hand, Sheila was short, stout, and light-skinned. Her brown hair was pulled back in a bun, and she sported white-framed glasses.

I pulled a file folder with duplicate printouts of Tim's phone records from my tote and handed it to Aaron. After he thanked me, he tucked the dossier under his notes. Since I hadn't followed protocol, they wouldn't be entered into evidence. Last night, I'd studied the documents and jotted down names to check out. Since I had some further work to do, I'd keep the list to myself for now.

Aaron brought the meeting to order. "Sheila, did you take care of the exterminator?"

"Yes, sir."

"Very good. The coroner released his final report. Nothing new. A copy is saved in the file folder on the server for your reference. The body will be released to the funeral home tomorrow."

My heart squeezed with the finality of that statement. Brad and Tim's brother could arrange for the cremation and the memorial service. I sent him a quick text with the news. "What are we supposed to say about the cause of death?"

"Drowning accident during the storm. Body just recently discovered."

I shuddered at Aaron's cold, clipped answer.

Aaron took a sip of coffee and then continued, "JP, please share your current theory on the money laundering."

"It is speculation. There is no solid proof at this point, but I suspect we are dealing with a ring of drug dealers that may be connected to the Corsican mafia. I believe the cartel preys on young men and women who are eager for easy money. In exchange for a paid vacation and a stipend, they agree to smuggle cash in their checked luggage. Once they arrive on the island, they put the money in a bag and pass it off to a courier. The broker then delivers the funds to businesses on the island that launder the money." On the drive over, JP had shared that Aaron wanted to keep the assumption that Dale was one of them between the three of us.

I heard a loud scratching on metal overhead and shivered. Must be some big rats. After I recovered, I said, "That sounds like what Tim alluded to in his story."

"Indeed, and your friend was correct. Certain airports are particularly lax with security around checked baggage. The agents are more concerned with weapons, illegal drugs, and explosives than other contraband."

"Well done." Aaron nodded toward JP. "It's a solid hypothesis. We'll need to gather more evidence before we obtain a search-and- seizure order to audit Ziggy's accounts. Felix and Sheila, the two of you will watch the comings and goings at the airport today. JP will coach you on what to look for." Aaron examined his handwritten notes. "Sheila, did you bring your list of possible sources of the pentobarbital?"

"Yes, sir." The stapled copies she passed around were three pages long. It would be difficult to identify the origin of the drug that killed Tim without more information.

"We'll table any further research for now. I want everyone to review and let me know if anything catches your eye." Aaron cleared his throat. "Here's the report on the evidence from the beach." He extracted papers from a folder and handed them out. "There were fibers on the bottom of the boat that matched the piece of cloth inside the vessel. If this is the boat the murderer used, the fabric may be what the body was wrapped in. No fingerprints, footprints, or DNA were left behind. There were traces of latex protein, so we can assume that the person wore gloves. The team also found remnants from what may have been shoe covers."

Whoever used the boat had covered their tracks. Although the theory tracked Tim's storyline, where was the direct link to Tim's murder? I studied the document. The name of a hotel and an identification number were on the back of the vessel. "Has anyone contacted the hotel?"

"I called this morning," Aaron replied. "They rent the boats out, and they discovered this one missing last Tuesday. The thief sawed the lock off the chain. We also received the report back on the bit of fabric Liz found on Mastic Trail. The traces of DNA were eroded, most likely due to the recent storms. Sheila and Felix, report your findings from yesterday's surveillance."

Felix went first. "Sir, for now I don't recommend allocating additional resources to search Mastic Trail. I found no signs of a struggle in the area."

"Point taken. We'll table that for now. Sheila?"

As she recounted her activities, I jiggled my legs. I wasn't used to sitting in meetings, and this one had droned on too long. I needed to work the case.

"Felix, has IT recovered the manuscript?" Aaron asked.

"No, sir. But they're working on it."

I snapped out of my meeting coma and said, "Tim copyrighted the story. He left the rights to Brad. I can see about getting another copy for the records. We also found a copy of his research notes on his Cloud account."

"Great news. I'll let you know if IT's efforts are unsuccessful," Aaron said. A thud resounded overhead, and Aaron lifted his face toward the ceiling. "Sounds like the exterminators are here." He doled out the day's assignments and adjourned the session.

JP and I hustled out of the conference room just in time for our breakfast rendezvous with the banker, Spencer. Would he provide additional insight into the island's nefarious activities?

Chapter 13

As JP and I walked the three short blocks to the restaurant, he said, "It is likely one or more of the local banks are involved in the scheme."

"How?"

"C'est possible that Ziggy deposits the cash with a bank and then wires the funds to foreign accounts. The financial industry is required to follow certain regulations, but for a cut, the regulators may turn the other way. My hope is that our banker, Spencer, provides a few leads to follow up on."

After we'd agreed on how we'd approach the conversation with him, JP asked, "What do you think about the evidence from the boat?"

"My gut says it's connected to Tim's murder."

He nodded in agreement and then held the door open for me. As we entered the restaurant, I spotted a man with a receding hairline in a nearby booth. I immediately recognized Spencer from his photo on the bank's website. When he stood, he towered over JP, which was a feat since JP was over six feet tall. His lanky frame was dressed in banker attire: black slacks, a long-sleeved white shirt, and a yellow-and-black-striped tie. After the introductions, he waited until I slid into the booth before taking his seat.

"Thank you for agreeing to meet with us." JP wriggled into my side of the booth.

"My pleasure." Spencer placed his hand over mine. "Liz, I'm so sorry about Tim. Please accept my condolences. I only knew Tim through Becky, but he was a fine man." He emphasized 'fine' with his clipped British accent.

I pulled my hand away. "Thank you." We'd just adjourned our meeting. How did he know already? "When did you find out about Tim's death?"

"Becky told me after the police questioned her. She's been very upset. Poor girl."

"You tell anyone else?" JP asked.

"No. I haven't even shared the information with my wife."

Was he telling the truth? I wished that Duke was with me.

JP leaned forward and said in a low growl, "As of this morning, Tim's death is public, but his murder is not. The cause of death is listed as an accidental drowning. It's critical to the investigation that you do not share what you know with anyone." He emphasized the last word.

"Of course. I would never hinder the work of the police." Spencer shook his head.

I noted that the gesture was in direct contradiction to his

statement. The server interrupted our conversation, and I did a quick study of the menu and then placed an order for a cinnamon apple crepe with a fat-burning smoothie. Maybe the two would cancel each other out.

After JP and Spencer ordered coffee and English breakfasts, I said, "I understand you helped Tim with research for his novel."

"Yes. The premise was quite interesting. Although that would never happen on this island." He dropped his gaze, picked up his napkin, and placed it on his lap.

"What do you mean?" I asked.

"Money laundering. I understand Cayman used to have a reputation, but that's changed." He sat taller and went on to explain all the regulations and safeguards that were in place.

As he shared his expertise and his opinion on illegal banking activities on other islands in the Caribbean, my mind drifted to Tim's novel. Checks and balances worked well unless collusion was involved. What if Spencer, Dale, and Ziggy were partners in crime?

When our food arrived, I asked, "Do you know Dale Foster?" JP elbowed my side under the table.

"The cop?" He wrinkled his brow.

I nodded as I sampled a bit of the thin fluffy pancake dusted with cinnamon and stuffed with a warm apple and caramel mixture.

"Yes. Of course. Why do you ask?" Spencer cut into his eggs and forked a bite.

"Did you know that he's the commissioner's cousin? Aren't there policies against nepotism?" I sipped the fat-burning smoothie and wrinkled my nose at the bitter, tangy taste of spinach and apple cider.

Spencer smirked. "It's a very small island, my dear," he said in a patronizing tone. "My brother works for me. We wouldn't be able to fill positions here otherwise."

JP turned the conversation back to the finance industry. As I half-listened, a plan formed in my head. I excused myself from the table and texted Becky.

Meet me for lunch in the park by your office. I'll bring salads and drinks. My treat.

She responded immediately.

Yay! What time?

Noon?

That works perfect with my lunch break. See you then.

When I rejoined the men, the conversation had turned to the bustling tourist industry. We finished our meals, and the waitress arrived with the check. JP pulled out his credit card, and Spencer slapped two fifty dollar bills on the table. "This one is on me."

After Spencer left, JP asked, "What was the Dale question about?"

"Just wanted to see how he'd react." I shrugged. " Um, can you interview the rest of the bankers on your own? I'd like to spend some time with Brad."

JP nodded. "D'accord. I shall be fine by myself. I will update you later."

I wasn't sure if he was disappointed or relieved.

~ * ~

Clouds rolled over the sun and granted a brief break from the midday heat. The breeze kept the temperatures bearable, while an umbrella-shaped tree shaded the picnic table in the small park. Becky approached. "Hi, Becky." I placed the takeout bag on the surface and extracted two boxes of jerk chicken salad.

"What's Duke doing here?" Becky had met my dog in Charleston when she attended our wedding as Tim's guest. After she took a seat on the bench, she gave him an awkward pat on the head.

I handed her a bottle of water and the provided utensils. "He rode on the plane with our friends. I thought Tim's dog, Snooper, might like some company, and we missed him."

"Oh." She pursed her lips as she considered my answer.

I rested my hand on her shoulder. "How are you doing?"

She hung her head and sniffled. "OK. Spencer's been a big help."

I removed my hand and parked myself across from her. Duke wagged his tail as I unboxed my lunch. "You told your bank president?" I chided her even though I knew the truth from my earlier conversation with Spencer.

Becky looked at me and grimaced. "I know I wasn't supposed to say anything. It's been so hard. I couldn't cope." Her hands shook as she uncapped the plastic container of vinaigrette and poured it over her salad.

"Sounds like you two are close." Were they having an affair?

"He's like a father to me."

I was relieved that Duke didn't yip.

As I savored the spicy meat and crunchy lettuce, Becky continued, "I still feel awful that the last time I saw Tim we fought."

"I never asked what you argued about."

"You saw how he treated me at your wedding." She stuck out her bottom lip. "He was more interested in that Sam girl than me. Tim said I was being silly and unreasonable, which only made it worse." She dabbed at the corner of her eyes with her napkin and averted my gaze. "I threw my coffee mug at him. It missed, but it shattered into a gazillion pieces. He stormed out and said he'd talk to me later . . . when I calmed down." Tears flowed down her cheeks, and she hiccupped.

I waited for her to continue.

"And then I went to work, and he ghosted me. Didn't return my calls or texts."

Duke yipped.

Was the yip because she never showed up for work that day, or was it because she had communicated with Tim? I made a mental note to double-check the phone records for the length of her calls. I wanted to ask her straight out if she murdered Tim, but instead I said, "Are you sure you didn't hear from him after that?"

"No, nothing. That cop, Aaron, asked me the same thing yesterday."

Not a sound from Duke.

"Aaron said I wasn't a suspect, but he asked a lot of questions. It was upsetting . . . well, until he told me that I was beautiful."

A slow grin spread across her face.

My PI hackles raised. Even though my dog hadn't yipped while she bawled, the quick shift in mood made me wonder if the tears were an act.

"He even asked me out, but he said we'd have to wait until the case was solved."

I dropped my fork. "He asked you for a date?"

"Yeah. I know it's probably too early. But he is kind of cute. I'm not sure cops make much money though."

"Probably not." She sure didn't seem like the grieving girlfriend that Spencer had described earlier.

"How's the honeymoon going?" She winked.

"Not exactly as planned." I stabbed a piece of lettuce with my fork.

"Oh, I almost forgot to tell you." Becky leaned forward. "I stopped by the shelter yesterday. Leonard got an agent. Can you believe it? He's confident she'll find a publisher for his book *Caribbean Capers*. Maybe even a movie deal. Isn't that exciting?"

Although the shelter's manager hadn't specified the stage of the manuscript when we visited, I was under the impression that Leonard had just started his book. If an agent was interested, they'd request the full story. "His manuscript is complete?"

"Yes. She's already received requests from several publishers for a full review. We're celebrating over drinks tomorrow night, and he's going to spill the details. He even gave me a copy of the first chapter to read."

"You're going out with creepy Leonard?"

"It's not a date, and he's just quirky. Probably because he has an author's imagination."

"If you say so." My phone pinged with a text from Brad.

The memorial service is on Thursday. Tim's brother will be here tomorrow.

That was fast.

I added a sad emoji.

Yeah. Jim wants to bring the ashes back for the second service.

My heart grew heavy, the ceremony that would take place in California. I fingered a question.

Any idea when that will be?

Probably a week from Saturday.

I prayed the case would be solved by then.

OK. Can you pick us up in thirty minutes?

Brad replied with a thumbs up. I set the device on the table. "Sorry. That was Brad. Tim's memorial service will be this Thursday."

Becky began to howl. Passers-by stopped and stared. I fetched tissues from my tote and handed them to her.

Duke whined.

When she finally calmed down, she said, "Is my face a wreck?"

I nodded. Her mascara-rimmed eyes resembled a raccoon.

"I need to fix my face before I go back to work." She stood and boxed up the remnants of her lunch.

Duke gazed longingly at the container hoping for a tidbit. I slipped him a piece of my chicken. "OK. I'll text you the details." Before she left, I hugged her.

While I finished my meal, I reflected on our conversation. She'd seemed genuinely upset, but Becky had also demonstrated that she was moody and had a temper. Afterall, she'd thrown a coffee mug at Tim and threatened to kill him at our reception. Had she murdered him? I wish that I'd asked her straight out while I had the chance.

I checked the time on my phone. Jax's funeral was in two hours.

~ * ~

The small non-denominational church in Georgetown was packed. By the time we arrived, only a few seats were left, so Brad and I elected to stand. Despite the air conditioning, the heat from the swarm of bodies was stifling, and I fanned my face with the program.

Rows of pews flanked the altar. As I scanned the crowd for familiar faces, I spotted Spencer with whom I assumed was his wife in the second row on the right-hand side. Ziggy sat behind him.

No sign of Dale or Becky. However, the commissioner was seated on the other side of Spencer's wife, and Lexie from the bar was next to Ziggy. Pearl sat on the opposite side with a few people I recognized from our visit to her home, including Jams.

Jax's family filled the first five rows marked reserved that faced the altar. In the front row was an older couple. A younger woman sat next to them. A blue porcelain urn stood center stage. Per the funeral program, Jax's ashes would be scattered at sea tomorrow at sunset.

Just before the ceremony began, Becky strolled in and took the seat next to Aaron. Her face had recovered from the earlier crying jag.

The choir started the ceremony with a sweet arrangement of "Amazing Grace." After the minister read a few passages, he invited individuals to share stories about Jax.

The older man from the front row approached the podium. His voice rang flat as he shared stories about his son and his involvement in the family business. His face displayed little emotion as two of the family members in the front pew sobbed. One of them had to be Jax's mom. The younger woman might have been his sister.

One of Jax's aunts spoke next, and then Ziggy stepped up to the pulpit. "Jax be a fine young man. He was a 'portant member of dis community." Ziggy spoke about how much he appreciated Jax's contributions to the local economy. He didn't elaborate.

Jax's cousin followed Ziggy. "My cousin loved to play basketball." He shared childhood memories spent shooting hoops and the days they'd skipped school to scuba dive off the coast.

I was surprised when Aaron took the stage. The connections on this island were more intricate than a spider's web.

Aaron began. "As a boy, I visited my aunt and cousin during the summers. I remember when I first met Jax at the local YMCA swimming pool. He was a brat." The audience chuckled. Aaron described that day and the relationship that developed over the years. When he returned to his seat, he placed an arm around a sniffling Becky.

The minister concluded the remembrance with a reading from the twenty-third Psalm and then invited everyone to the celebration of life at Lizard Lounge. The ceremony concluded with Mariah Carey's "One Sweet Day."

"Do you think we should attend the reception?" I asked Brad. We barely knew the man.

"Yes. No one will know the difference, and we have an open invitation from Lexie. Why not?"

If it could bring us closer to Tim's killer, I was all in. "OK. Let's go."

~ * ~

Outside, a small group gathered in the smoking area. The breeze blew the stench of cigarettes indoors. All the seats at the bar were taken, so I snagged a table by the restroom and waited while Brad fetched our drinks. A long buffet table hugged the opposite wall. People placed chips, dips, and various other potluck dishes that they'd brought to the occasion on the table. Pearl stopped to say hello before she added her fruit salad to the mix.

"I'm sorry 'bout your friend." She set the Tupperware bowl down and patted my hand.

"Thank you."

"Murdered." She shook her head.

His obituary claimed that it was a tragic accidental drowning during the storm. "How'd you find out?"

"Honey, Ms. Pearl she hears dese tings." She tapped the side of her ear with her finger.

"Don't you worry dat pretty lil head of yours. Not many folks know what Pearl know."

I recalled that she was the queen of the island's rumor mill. "Pearl, what's the deal with Jax's dad? He didn't shed a tear, and I haven't seen him since the service."

Pearl's eyes scanned the room. "I can't tell you now." She leaned closer and whispered, "You folk find dat treasure?"

"We found the spot, but someone else had already dug it up."

Pearl's shoulders slumped, and she frowned. "Didn't hear dat. Wonder who got it."

"What do you know about the history of Blackbeard's treasure and the island?"

"Lordy, more den I can tell ya' today. Youse two come see me soon."

As Brad returned with two glasses of the house red in fresh plastic glasses, Pearl picked up her dish. "I'd bettah set dis on da table."

"What was that about?" Brad handed me my wine.

"Somehow she found out that Tim was murdered. Oh, and she wants us to visit her. She has some history on Blackbeard." I searched the crowd for Becky and then remembered that tonight was her non-date with Leonard. While I was thinking about it, I shot her a quick text. Leonard's book weighed on my mind.

Have fun on your date.

Ha-ha.

Any chance I can read the pages Leonard gave you?

Why?

Just curious.

I'll bring them with me tomorrow.

Thanks.

I set the phone down and placed my hands on the ache in my chest. Tomorrow. Tim's memorial service.

Tim had been very specific about the details in his will. The ceremony would take place on the stretch of beach behind his house. Although he hadn't shared his faith with me, it was reflected in the short speech that he asked to be read at the celebration of his life. The occasion would be infused with champagne, music, food, and dance. Tim's brother and sister-in law were due to arrive in a few hours and would stay at the house with Jenny and Lawson.

Brad nudged my arm. "Here comes Ziggy."

"My, my . . . How youse twos know Jax?"

I took a sip of sour wine and set the plastic cup on the table. "We're here to pay respects on behalf of our friend Tim."

"Saw the obit in the Cayman Compass dis morn. Thought you said he be found." Ziggy didn't wait for a response. "Guess dat book'll nevah be published."

Brad clenched his jaw and then narrowed his eyes. "It sure as hell will be," he growled. "Tim left the copyright to me. His life's work will be in the hands of readers. You can bet the island on that."

Ziggy took a long swig from his bottle of Caybrew. "Whatcha mean copyright?"

"It means the story is protected. *And I have the rights to it.* That book will be out before you know it."

A few seconds passed before Ziggy said, "Well ain't dat be fine. I'm gonna check out da food."

I noted that Ziggy walked in the opposite direction of the buffet and directly toward Spencer. After a short conversation, Spencer glanced our way, picked up his phone, and went outside.

Chapter 14

Tim's brother, Jim, broke down in grief the moment he stepped inside the house he would inherit. I couldn't imagine the regret he must have felt that this was his first visit to his brother's home. His wife Michelle followed and sneezed as she crossed the doorstep.

"I'm sorry," I said. "I forgot you're allergic. We can board the pets first thing tomorrow."

"No. As long as I take my allergy medication, I'll be OK. If you don't mind showing us to our room, I'll take my medicine now, so it doesn't get any worse."

While Jim and Michelle settled in, I fed the pets, let the dogs do their business, and then shut them in our bedroom. Duke and Snooper protested with barks, while Irish curled up on a pillow on the bed.

Brad uncorked a bottle of white wine, and I assembled a tray with an assortment of cheeses and crackers.

"This place is incredible," Michelle said as the couple joined us in the kitchen.

"Yeah. I wish we'd come here sooner." Jim's face was etched with regret.

"Why don't we go outside?" I offered. "You can meet Jenny and Lawson and experience your first Cayman sunset."

When we stepped outdoors, Michelle's jaw dropped, and she snapped a few pictures of the scenery with her phone. I set the plate of snacks on the glass-top table and took a seat across from Jenny.

"It's nice, isn't it?" I said after Michelle joined us.

"Nice is an understatement. The gray porcelain tiles, the stainless steel outdoor kitchen, the view of the water. It's amazing."

"Tim sent me a few pictures after he moved in, but the photos didn't do this place justice." Jim placed a slice of smoked Gouda on a club cracker. "I understand you're helping the police with their investigation. I still can't believe that someone murdered my brother. Do you really think it was because of the book he wrote?"

"Probably. But there are other possible motives."

"Like what?" Michelle asked.

"Jealousy. Greed."

Jim slammed his fist on the arm of his chair, startling us all. "I hope whoever did this pays."

"Honey . . ." Michelle caressed his arm.

Lawson stroked his goatee. "I keep wondering who snatched the treasure, and if it's connected."

"What treasure?" Jim asked.

Brad filled the couple in on Tim's note, the map, and our search for the goods. "He intended the shared adventure to be our wedding gift. But when we followed the map, we discovered someone else had already dug it up."

Michelle swallowed a sip of her chardonnay. "Fascinating. Do you think there was an actual treasure chest? I wonder what was in it."

"Probably full of this." Brad produced the gold coin we'd found and showed it to Jim and Michelle.

Jenny's eyes lit up as she shared the research that she'd conducted on the island's pirates and her theory on the source of the piece. "The coin is identical to the ones found in Blackbeard's treasure on Cayman Brac." She went on to explain the pirate's history and his ties to both the Caymans and Charleston, South Carolina. "I wrote a history paper on him in high school."

"What was your paper about?" Michelle asked.

"About how he blockaded the Charleston port in the 1700s." She leaned forward. "I had to go to the Deep Web to find this out. Rumor has it that Blackbeard had an illegitimate son named Edward with a Jamaican woman on Grand Cayman."

"Edward is Blackbeard's real name," I said.

"Right." Jenny nodded. "Apparently, the pirate was quite fond of his only son. He gifted him part of the treasure, so he'd never have to work a day of his life. The boy buried it for safekeeping. He died of yellow fever before he turned eighteen."

"How sad," Michelle said.

"And you believe the treasure Tim found was part of Edward's buried loot?" Brad asked.

"That's my theory. I'm researching the ancestry to locate any living relatives."

Jim asked, "How is it connected to Tim's murder?"

"There's no evidence that it is," I said.

He shook his head. "My brother led an interesting life."

We all grew silent as we contemplated Jim's comment.

~ * ~

Last night, after we'd polished off two large pepperoni pizzas, Jim and Michelle retired to bed. While Brad and I cleaned up the dinner dishes, we'd decided to give the couple the house to themselves for a few hours tomorrow. Brad and I planned to rent bikes and cycle the Cayman Sunrise trail. I gently reminded him that it was a tourist ride and not a leg of a triathlon. Jenny and Lawson wanted to take the dogs to Collier's public beach.

The next day, after my morning meeting, we dropped the gang off and then drove to the east end.

"Anything new on the investigation?" Brad asked.

"Sheila and Felix tailed a suspicious young couple from the airport. They dropped off their luggage at a condo complex and then drove into Georgetown. Same routine. Dale picked up the duffle bag they left behind and then delivered it to Ziggy's place."

"Sounds like Ziggy's cleaning some cash."

"Oh, and one of the bankers that JP interviewed didn't think Spencer was on the up-and-up. But who knows, could be professional jealousy."

"Is the team getting any closer to figuring out who killed Tim?"

There were too many loose ends and possible motives to answer yes. "We've gathered a lot of evidence. I'm hoping something breaks soon."

~ * ~

We started our bike ride at Hidden Family Cave. One of the many networks of caverns on the island. A group of tourists stood at the entrance of the limestone catacombs. I listened as the guide expounded on the history and the rumors that pirates had buried treasure deep within the rocks. After I snapped a few pictures, I pedaled fast to catch up with Brad. "Um, could you slow down a little?" I huffed.

"Don't worry about me. There's a nice wilderness section at the end of the trail. Plenty of tourists around. How 'bout we meet up there afterward if we lose track of each other?" As he sped away, I glared at his back. The man wasn't even winded. And what happened to him not wanting me to go anywhere alone?

I cycled past the rock steps that led to Lighthouse Park. When I spotted the marker for the blowholes on the side of the trail, I gave up any attempt to keep up with Brad and parked my bike. As I descended the stairs to the beach, waves slapped the shoreline, and white foam gushed into the air. While I admired the natural phenomenon, I navigated the stony shore with the other tourists to get a better photo. Mist from the spray of water blew across my body. As I steadied my hand to snap a picture with my phone, someone pushed me from behind, and I fell to the rocky shore.

A man's voice growled, "This is your last warning. Quit poking around where ya' don't belong." He spat on the ground next to me.

I scrambled for my phone, which fortunately had landed in a patch of sand. Blood poured from my knees where I'd landed on jagged rocks. I turned around and snapped a picture of the man's back as he ran up the stairs.

"Are you OK? I saw what that guy did to you." A young Jamaican woman offered me her hand. "Oh my God, your legs," she exclaimed. "I'm a nurse. Can I dress your legs for you?"

"Please," I pleaded. "Did you happen to get a good look at the guy who did this?"

"I'm sorry. I was too busy watching the water. He was wearing a hoodie. I wish I had more, but I don't." She extracted bandages and alcohol wipes from her backpack. "I hope you don't mind Disney princess Band-Aids. My six-year-old insists on them."

"Not at all." I winced as she wiped my wounds and then bandaged them.

"You OK?" she repeated.

"Yeah. I'll be fine." I clasped her hands. "I can't thank you enough for your help."

Before I mounted my bike, I considered calling Brad and then dismissed the thought. What could he do now? Nothing. The bleeding had subsided. Besides, I was furious with him for leaving me behind. While I pedaled, I considered the warning. What had triggered it, and who was behind it?

When I arrived at our rendezvous point, I sighed. White

herons peacefully perched on dead branches that jutted out of the glass-like surface of Collier's Pond. A family of blue-winged teals glided across the water. A long-legged, black-necked stilt feasted on insects on the pond's surface, and black-throated blue warblers dotted branches in the shrubs. I spotted Brad seated on a bench at the far end of the pond.

After I parked my bike, he asked, "What happened to your legs?"

I considered a super snarky comment before I replied with the facts. "Another threat. Someone pushed me. A good Samaritan stopped and tended to my wounds."

Brad's jaw dropped. His response was tormented. "I'm sorry. I shouldn't have left you behind."

Damn straight. But I let it go. Brad was struggling with the loss of his friend. He deserved a pass.

~ * ~

The sound of Tim's front doorbell woke me up at ten. I dragged myself out of bed and peered out the window. The rental tables and chairs had arrived. The funeral home had arranged for the rentals, the catering, the flowers, and the music.

We'd decided to stay at the house so that we could help Jim and Michelle with the preparations for the celebration of Tim's life. I'd tossed and turned before I'd finally fallen asleep around seven in the morning. The ceremonies would begin at one this afternoon.

When the doorbell rang for a second time and the flower delivery arrived, I meandered to the kitchen to brew a cup of tea and then escaped to our room. Since Aaron had excused me from the morning meeting, I propped up some pillows on the bed and spread out my notes in front of me. Duke hopped up on the other side.

What had set off the last verbal warning? I reflected on the conversation at Lizard Lounge. Ziggy seemed shocked that a copy of Tim's story still existed. What if Ziggy, Dale, and Spencer murdered Tim to ensure the book was never published? Was Dale aware of the money laundering investigation that his cousin was conducting? Or was Aaron in on it too? Did the commissioner plan to derail the team's efforts so that the perps were never brought to justice? Since JP was involved, I didn't think so, but I wasn't ready to rule out the possibility. And then there was Becky. I couldn't imagine her being that calculated, but I wasn't ready to scratch her off the list . . . yet.

Who would have preferred the method that was used to kill Tim, and where did they source the drug? Dale fit that profile. He was familiar with police procedures and investigation scenes.

My mentor Gunner's wise teachings popped into my head. Follow the money. What about the buried treasure? Was it connected, and had anyone shown signs of a recent windfall? I scratched the back of my head. Was I getting any closer? When I had a chance, I'd call Gunner and Sam. I needed an outsider's perspective.

Duke jumped off the bed as soon as Brad entered the room. "Liz, you better get ready. It's almost noon."

Yikes. Brad adjusted his shirt in the mirror. He fiddled with the buttons and then pulled his belt one notch tighter. Had he lost weight?

Before I headed for the shower, I stuffed my notes in a drawer and embraced my husband in a bear hug.

After I'd donned the one black dress that I'd brought and tended to the pets, I put Snooper, Duke, and Irish in our bedroom. Irish promptly hid under the bed.

I stepped outside and searched for Brad. The funeral home had set up a large white tent on the beach to offer protection from the sun. Pots of fuchsia bougainvillea framed the structure. Servers stood at each entrance and offered flutes of champagne. Notes of instrumental reggae music carried in the breeze. I was amazed at how quickly they put the event together. As I scanned the scene, someone nudged my elbow. I turned.

"Hi, Becky."

She wore a black halter dress that hugged her frame and showed off a little too much cleavage.

"I wanted to give you this before everything starts." She handed me a manila envelope. She must've noticed my puzzled look because she added, "It's Leonard's manuscript."

"Oh, right. Thank you for bringing it." I tucked it under my arm. "How'd it go last night?"

"OK. Leo should be here soon. His agent found a publisher and negotiated a big advance. Isn't that exciting?"

"I guess." Leo, really?

She leaned forward and lowered her voice. "He also wants to buy Tim's house."

"Why?" I shook my head as I tried to process her comment. "Never mind." I needed to put the package away and find Brad.

"He'll need to talk to Tim's brother about that. And today is not the best time." The advance from the publisher must have been a sizeable sum. "Thank you for this." I patted the envelope. "I'm going to put it inside. I'll see you in a few minutes."

After I'd placed the document in my tote, I went back out to join the celebration of Tim's life. I entered the tent and found Brad. He'd ditched the sport coat he wore earlier. The sun bore down, and even with the covering and the chillers, the temperature inside the structure grew warm. I counted over seventy people. Tim had made a lot of friends during his brief time on the island. I spotted some familiar faces, the neighbors, Spencer and his wife, Lexie from the bar, Leonard, and Wendy, the shelter's receptionist. JP and Aaron had also come to pay their respects. No Dale or Ziggy.

Inside the tent, the funeral home had installed a large piece of plywood over the sand. Round tables that seated six surrounded a dance stage. Soon the band would start playing. Tim had been clear in his will that he didn't want a eulogy or folks behind a mike recounting memories. Just a simple speech he'd written and then everyone could mix and mingle.

Along one side of the tent was a sprawling buffet table ladened with an eclectic mix of Tim's favorite foods, chilled shrimp and fresh conch marinated in lime juice, breakfast tacos, lobster mac and cheese, prime rib with horseradish sauce, asparagus with hollandaise sauce, garlic mashed potatoes, crab stuffed mushrooms, and every chocolate dessert you could imagine. I found a spot close to the stage and watched as people piled their plates with food and found their seats.

Brad had agreed to read the note Tim wrote for his friends and family. Jim didn't think he could do it. As Brad stepped up to the microphone, he cleared his throat. "I want to thank you all for coming. Many of you don't know me, but I'm Brad, Tim's former business partner and best friend." His voice hitched. "He left a short note and requested that it be shared with the people he loved."

"Today is a day of celebration. I've chosen my favorite foods and music to share with you. Live each day, follow your dreams, and have faith in the Lord. Cheers."

Tears escaped from Brad's eyes as he raised his glass. I heard an audible sob from Becky and prayed she wouldn't make a scene. After Brad stepped away from the mike, the band began to play "Three Little Birds," by Bob Marley and the Wailers.

I closed my eyes and swayed to the music. Brad draped his arm over my shoulder, and we moved together to the tune. I extracted a tissue from the pocket of my dress and wiped away the teardrops that streamed down my cheeks.

As Becky and Leonard stepped onto the stage to dance, I turned away in disgust and tugged on Brad's sleeve. "Let's get something to eat."

JP sat with Aaron at a table close to the buffet. We waved at them as we passed. Once we loaded our plates with food, we joined Jim and Michelle at a table away from the stage.

"I hate that this is happening," Jim said. "But my brother did it right . . . the music, the food, the speech. Thank you for delivering it, Brad."

"It was a privilege," Brad replied.

We ushered the last of the crowd out at six p.m. Workers deconstructed the tent and loaded the contents onto their trucks. We all changed into more comfortable clothes. I let the pets out to do their business and then fed them. Although I was a little tipsy, I poured myself a generous glass of wine and joined Jenny, Lawson, Brad, Jim, and Michelle on the patio. The sun sank into the sea while a full moon shone overhead.

"The celebration was beautiful," Michelle commented.

"Cheers to Tim." Brad's voice choked on the words as he raised his champagne. We all clinked glasses.

"And cheers to his book. May he live on through it," I added.

"Yeah." Jim choked back a sob.

Snooper and Duke provided some comic relief as they hunted for lizards in the bushes.

"What's going to happen to Tim's pets?" Michelle asked.

Jenny's face beamed. That girl could light up a room. "Well, if it's ok with you all, I'd like to adopt them."

Lawson frowned, but Jenny ignored his obvious misgivings.

Michelle placed her hand on Jim's. "Honey, that's a good solution."

"You'll let us know how they're doing?" Jim asked.

"Of course." They exchanged contact information.

I yawned and nearly toppled my glass of wine.

Brad kissed my cheek. "Sweetheart, why don't you go to bed? It's been a long day."

That was an understatement.

I was emotionally exhausted. "Good idea. Goodnight all." I stood and blew a kiss to the group before I headed inside.

Duke was too enamored with Snooper to follow me.

Chapter 15

The next morning, the bright sunlight that streamed through the blinds woke me. Duke snored softly by my side of the bed. I patted the space next to me. Where was Brad? And what time was it? I checked my phone, nine a.m. I'd slept over twelve hours and missed the morning meeting at the station.

After I'd scrubbed my face free of yesterday's make-up and put on a robe, I followed the scent of freshly brewed coffee into the kitchen. Michelle and Jim were seated at the kitchen table eating breakfast. Brad, Lawson, and Jenny were absent.

"Help yourself." Michelle gestured toward the scrambled eggs and bacon on the countertop.

"Where is everybody?" I asked.

"Lawson and Jenny took Snooper for a walk. I haven't seen Brad this morning," Jim responded.

"Maybe he went for a run." I poured myself a generous cup of joe. I needed extra caffeine.

Scratching sounded from the ceiling, followed by a faint chirp.

"What's that noise? I heard it last night too," Michelle asked.

"According to Becky, Tim has bats in the attic." I recalled the noted appointment on Tim's calendar. "Pest control is scheduled for this weekend."

Jim ran his hand through his hair. "I guess I'll need to hire a property manager to take care of this place."

"I have some names that the neighbors gave me."

"Thanks. That'd be great," Jim replied.

I left to fetch the notes from my tote and then jotted the information down for Jim. After I handed him the list, I made another pot of coffee and poured myself a cup. As time passed, I began to pace the room. I texted Brad. No answer. When I called him, the phone went to voice mail. My stomach dropped.

I excused myself and fetched Duke from our bedroom. While we combed the property, I scanned the outer landscape. Duke whined when we approached the trash cans. "What's up, boy?" The lid of one bin sat open, and a bag was left on the ground. I hefted the bag up and dropped it in the can. A paper towel escaped from a small opening at the top. "Darn varmints." I picked the trash up, threw it in the bin, and closed the lid.

After a fruitless search, we returned to the house without Brad. Lawson and Jenny had joined Jim and Michelle in the kitchen.

"Guys, I'm worried. I can't find Brad."

"Maybe he went for a run or a bike ride?" Lawson suggested.

"I checked the grounds for him, and Tim's two bikes and the Jeep are still in the garage." Although my brain was foggy, my gut told me something was amiss. The behavior wasn't like Brad. He would've at least given me a kiss before he departed. "Has anyone seen him this morning?"

No one had seen him since last night. "Do you know what time he went to bed?" I asked. "I was out like a light. I never even heard him come into our room."

"We all went to bed around midnight," Jenny replied. "He said he was going to start the dishwasher and then call it a night."

I stepped outside, placed a call to JP, and explained the situation. The sun bore down on my neck.

"Perhaps he needed some time to himself?" he offered.

"No. I'm telling you something is wrong." I struggled to keep the panic out of my voice.

"D'accord. I will come and get you. We will find him."

An hour later, Duke and I piled into JP's car, "Thank you for helping me."

"De rien. When was he last seen?"

"I went to bed early last night, but everyone else stayed up until midnight. I fell sound asleep, so I have no idea if he even came to our room. I asked the others, and no one remembers seeing him after they all went to bed. JP, I'm worried."

"Where should we start?"

I recalled the exchange between Ziggy and Spencer at Lizard Lounge after Brad divulged his determination to publish Tim's story.

"Ziggy's," I said without hesitation.

Duke hung his head out the back window of JP's vehicle. His tongue flopped in the wind. "Why Ziggy's?" JP asked.

"Maybe he's responsible for Brad's disappearance. My gut says Ziggy's involved somehow."

In the back, Duke whined.

"C'est possible. Perhaps we should drive around Tim's neighborhood first. Maybe he is out for a long walk."

"No. The last tours will have already gone out by the time we get there. The clock's ticking. If Brad went for a walk, I'll get a phone call when he returns to the house."

"Ma chérie." He hesitated. "He may be injured. Maybe he was hit by a car."

I closed my eyes and prayed that Brad was OK. "I'll call the hospitals on the way."

JP focused on the road, while I made phone calls. None of the hospitals had admitted a patient named Brad O'Connor or anyone who fit his description.

"What's our plan when we arrive?" JP asked.

"Ziggy doesn't like Duke. I say we confront him. Threaten to sic my dog on him if he doesn't cooperate."

"Liz, we need to follow protocol. After all, we do not have any evidence that Ziggy is connected to his disappearance."

My face flushed. We'd come to this island to celebrate our honeymoon, then our friend was murdered, and now my husband was MIA. "Screw protocol. We need to find Brad, and my gut says Ziggy's involved."

Ever patient, JP sighed "Tell me more about this gut feeling you have."

I explained what happened after Jax's funeral. "Spencer and Ziggy want the book, and they know Brad has the copyright. I don't see Spencer getting his hands dirty. That's why my gut says Ziggy nabbed him."

"Fair enough. It is a good theory. So, you believe that they want Brad to transfer the rights?"

"Yes." I groaned in frustration.

"But they would need a solicitor for that. Perhaps they have taken him to a law firm."

"Maybe. But Ziggy wouldn't abandon his business during tourist hours, so his shop is a good place to start."

"D'accord," JP conceded. "But we will survey the area before we barge in. You have your weapon?"

"Yes." I stared out the window and focused on the job ahead of us.

JP parked the car in the back of the lot underneath a clump of palm trees. I clipped Duke's leash to his collar. "Find Brad," I whispered in my dog's ear. We headed toward the pier. Most of the boats were out on tours. Duke kept his nose to the ground.

"Let's check out the buildings in the back," JP said.

As we approached, Duke sniffed the air and then lunged forward.

"He's picked up on a scent," I said.

"Liz, wait."

It took all my might to rein my dog in. "What?"

"Draw your piece. Who knows what we will find ahead."

I carefully extracted the pistol from my tote while keeping a strong arm on the leash. "Got it." My heart hammered in my ears as Duke tugged me forward. As we approached a red-and-white wooden shack, Duke whined. "Shush," I hushed him.

JP whispered, "You go first. If Brad is in there with Ziggy, it's best Ziggy believes it's only you and Duke. I will be right behind you, prepared to take a shot if needed. Be careful, ma chérie."

Once I'd confirmed that JP had his weapon drawn, I gently turned the door handle and raised my weapon. Unlocked. I pulled the door open. The small space was filled with life jackets and snorkel equipment. In the far corner, Brad stood behind a couple of stacked boxes with a pen in his hand. Spencer and Ziggy flanked him. Ziggy had a gun pointed at Brad's head.

"Well, ain't dis special. Now we have da newlyweds together." Ziggy aimed his piece at me next. "Drop it and get inside."

Duke whined.

As I dropped my gun, I locked eyes with Brad. I mouthed the word *duck*, and he dropped to the ground. Seconds later, a bullet whizzed by my side and grazed Ziggy's wrist. His gun tumbled to the floor, and I heard Spencer scramble for it. Brad beat him to it and picked up the weapon.

"Good shot," I said to JP as I retrieved my pistol from the floor.

Blood dripped onto the paper Brad was about to sign. Ziggy recovered from the shock and bellowed a string of cuss words.

"Thanks. Liz, point your weapon at Spencer. Brad, you take Ziggy while I cuff these two."

"The charges will never stick," Spencer said as JP snapped the handcuffs on his wrists. Once both men were cuffed, I passed Duke's leash to Brad, slipped on gloves, and bagged Ziggy's gun and the legal document they were coercing Brad to sign.

I placed the evidence in my tote and then embraced my husband.

"You two got here in the nick of time. I was just about to sign the rights away."

As I considered all the things that could have gone wrong, I shuddered.

Brad nodded toward JP. "Thanks, man."

"You are welcome." After JP phoned Aaron, he tied a handkerchief around Ziggy's wound. "Shall we take these felons to the station?"

Duke and Brad sat up front with JP, while I sat in the back of the sedan with the perps. When Ziggy spat on my leg, Duke growled. I couldn't wait to bring these scumbags to justice for the ordeal they'd put us through.

"What happened?" I asked Brad.

"I was taking out the trash, and some idiot chloroformed me. I woke up bound and gagged in the building where you found me." Brad drew long sips from the bottle of water JP handed him.

So, it was solved, sort of. Spencer and Ziggy had murdered Tim to prevent his novel from being published. I assumed that meant the two of them were somehow connected to the broader money laundering investigation. Once they'd found out that a copy of the manuscript still existed, they'd kidnapped Brad and attempted to coerce him into giving up the rights. We still didn't know the extent of Dale's role in the scheme. Was he the one responsible for the disappearance of the files from the server at the station?

Something was looming at the back of my mind. I just didn't know what.

When we arrived at the station, the commissioner greeted us. While the police booked Spencer and Ziggy, Brad and I headed to separate rooms to give officers our statements. As Duke and I strolled along the hallway, I spotted Dale. He glanced over his shoulder and darted out an exit. I sprinted after him.

Once we were outside, I unsnapped Duke's leash and pointed at Dale. "Get him." My dog sped toward the dirty cop and slammed into his back with his front paws. The force pushed Dale flat to the ground and knocked the wind out of him.

Before Dale recovered, Aaron joined us and planted his polished shoe in the middle of his cousin's shoulder blades. "Leaving early? I think not. I suspect you'll want to come with us back inside." Dale grunted, and Aaron pressed harder. "If you cooperate, I'll go easy on you. Or do I need to cuff you and embarrass you in front of the entire force?"

"Damn it, cuz. I'll cooperate. Can you take your foot off my back?" Aaron released his hold, and Dale stood and brushed the gravel off his hands. "Stupid dog," he murmured.

"Good boy." I patted Duke's head.

Aaron grabbed Dale's elbow and escorted him inside. Duke

and I followed. Aaron stopped and turned. "I can't thank you and Duke enough, Liz. Please give your statement and then go rest. I officially excuse you from this investigation. You've had a long day. I'll have a check waiting for you before you leave."

A war waged inside my mind. The PI in me wanted to see this through to the end, but hadn't life just taught me a lesson? My husband had been kidnapped and almost killed. The adrenaline drained from my body. Aaron was right. It'd been a long day, and we needed to enjoy some time on the island.

~ * ~

After we'd lavished love on Duke for finding Brad and detaining Dale, we'd left him at Tim's and returned to the hotel. Our celebration in the resort's dining room was bittersweet. Yes, we'd brought the perps to justice, but Tim was gone, and in a few days, we'd attend his second funeral in California.

Arched windows provided sweeping views of yet another stunning Caribbean sunset. A candle flickered and cast shadows on the white tablecloth. I regretted that this was our first visit to the hotel's restaurant.

"What's bothering you?" Brad topped off my wine.

I swirled the liquid and then inhaled the citrus scent. "Besides the fact that I could've lost you?"

He waited for me to continue.

"I'm not convinced that those guys murdered Tim. Yes, they wanted the manuscript, but I don't know . . . something about the sequence of events is off."

My phone pinged with a text from JP.

Dale, Spencer, and Ziggy claimed that they did not kill Tim. Dale confessed that he'd orchestrated the warning bullet and messages, but you still need to watch your backs.

I thought about JP's response and wondered why Dale had targeted me.

Why did he warn us and nobody else?

Based on his responses, I surmised that he believed he could control both his cousin and me. You were the outsider. He wanted you off the island.

I read the text to Brad. "Part of me wants to continue to investigate, and another part is kicking myself for getting involved in the first place. I put you, Jenny, and Lawson in danger."

Brad placed his hand over mine. "You didn't put us in danger. The criminals did. This is what you do, and I'm proud of you and Duke for taking Ziggy, Spencer, and Dale down." He rubbed my wrist with his thumb. "And you know what, I like JP. I'm sorry for being such an ass."

A young man dressed in black placed a plate of twin lobster tails accompanied by a bowl of garlic-infused butter on my placemat. Brad's filet mignon topped with crab smelled enticing. "Share?" Suddenly I was ravenous.

"Sure."

I exchanged a lobster tail for a portion of my husband's steak and then raised my glass. "Cheers."

"Cheers." His gaze caressed my face. "I love you, Liz Adams O'Connor." His eyes hardened. "If you're not done with this, I'm with you one hundred percent. I need to know that Tim's killer will be locked up for life."

I swallowed a gulp of wine. "OK. Tomorrow I'll review my notes. Maybe I'll find something. Let's enjoy tonight."

Chapter 16

Brad kissed my cheek before he left for his morning run. As I reviewed my notes, I recalled my conversation with Aaron. After he chastised me for the off-duty phone call, he shared the conversation he had with Dale. His cousin had thrown both Spencer and Ziggy under the bus. However, he'd insisted that none of them murdered Tim. Dale confessed that he'd eavesdropped on our team's meetings from the air ducts overhead. Guess the rats were of the human species. Aaron confirmed that his cousin had been behind all the warnings.

Dale thought he'd eliminated all copies of the story until we informed Ziggy that it was copyrighted. As soon as Spencer discovered the manuscript still existed, he orchestrated the kidnapping, and Ziggy waited for the right opportunity to carry out their plans.

Once Aaron swore me to secrecy, he divulged some of the details Dale revealed concerning the broader investigation. In a hushed tone, he explained that JP's theory about the laundering was correct. An international drug ring recruited young people from key hubs around the world. In exchange for first-class plane tickets, an all-expense paid trip, and a small stipend, the recruits smuggled the dirty money in vacuum-sealed packages hidden in secret compartments in their checked luggage.

Capital Management LLC, the firm that owned the condo across from our hotel, also owned the unit that Lisa and Tara had occupied. Aaron said the company was likely a shell organization and yet another method to launder the funds.

The bag that the girls delivered to Dale contained one million dollars of dirty cash. Grand Cayman wasn't the only Caribbean island involved in the operation.

After the dirty funds were delivered to tourist businesses and restaurants, the bills were commingled with clean bills. The establishments in question all had accounts at Spencer's bank. Since the organizations were known to deal in cash transactions, the large deposits of money weren't deemed suspicious.

The businesses then periodically wired the funds to designated offshore accounts per the instructions provided by their money courier. Aaron said it was likely the transactions were layered. He went on to explain the meaning of the term. After the initial bank received the wire, the money was then transferred to other legitimate accounts to avoid detection of the origin of the funds. Sounded like a shell game to me. Aaron and JP believed the money trail would eventually lead back to the Corsican mafia.

Since Spencer's brother was the bank's Money Laundering Reporting Officer, he made sure that any suspicious wire transactions went unreported. In exchange for ignoring the activity that the institution was required to disclose by law, both men received a substantial sum of cash that they then used to pay for various goods on the island. Aaron and JP were in the process of involving the appropriate authorities, and the case would likely take years to unravel.

The complexity of the scheme made my head spin. I prayed that this time JP would be able to prosecute the crooks.

After we ended the call, I phoned my mentor, Gunner, and relayed the facts surrounding Tim's murder. "It's too tidy," I said. "I'm not sure we've found the true culprit in his death."

He replied, "You have good instincts. Follow them."

As I contemplated Gunner's response, I fixed myself a cup of hot tea and then pulled up Sam's number.

"Girl, aren't you on your honeymoon? You should be having wild sex, not calling me."

"I wish." I explained everything that had transpired.

"Damn. That's some bad luck. Aside from Becky, Ziggy, Spencer, Dale, and Aaron, are there any outliers? Anyone who might have motive and means that you haven't considered?"

As I contemplated her question, I logged into my computer. I was grateful to discover that I still had access to the investigation team's shared folder.

Who else might have wanted Tim dead? Greed and envy were powerful motivators. While I sipped my tea, I opened the autopsy report and reread the contents. As I studied the medical examiner's notes, a small detail stood out. There were burn marks on Tim's neck. The kind that might be left behind by a taser.

I recalled the electric shock device on top of the counter at the shelter. Then I remembered Leonard's chapter. In the whirlwind of events since Brad's kidnapping, I'd forgotten to read his story. After I pulled the blinds, I fetched the papers from my bag. When I read the first two sentences, my jaw dropped.

"Secrets swirled in the island breeze. Some were harmless, like the sixteen-year-old girl who never told her parents that she skipped school to sneak off to a book signing event featuring her favorite author. And some could get you killed."

Word for word, it was Tim's thriller. A theory began to form in my mind. While the pieces of the puzzle clicked into place, Brad returned from his run.

"I need you to see something." I handed him the document. "Leonard did it." I told Brad about the autopsy report and the marks on Tim's neck.

After he read the chapter, Brad put his hand over his heart and then drew me close. "I knew you could solve it."

When we pulled apart, I wiped a stray tear from my eye. "I think as soon as Tim returned home, Leonard tased him. Then he administered the drug and dumped him in the sea."

Brad winced, but I pressed on. This was it. I knew it in my bones. "The pieces are coming together. . .the way he's been making the moves on Becky, his background . . . but I don't believe it's enough to nail him. We need more evidence." I tugged on my ear.

Brad passed the story back to me. "Like what?"

"I have an idea. Are you with me on this?"

"All the way."

I phoned JP and shared my suspicion.

~ * ~

When JP, Brad, and I arrived at the shelter, JP remained in the vehicle until the coast was clear. Around the corner two cops in an unmarked sedan awaited in case we needed back-up. Aaron remained at the station entangled in the money laundering case. I was equipped with a recording device and ready to roll. While Brad and I confronted Leonard and attempted to elicit a full confession, JP would be on stand-by in the reception area. Once we'd secured Leonard's admission of guilt, JP would move in for the arrest. If things went south, our code word was 'Secret.'

As Brad and I strode toward the rescue's entrance, Wendy exited the building and turned the key in the door. "I'm sorry, guys. We're closed. I'm just locking up."

"Is Leonard here?" I asked.

"Yes, he's in the back. He doesn't usually leave until around six."

Brad said, "Can we talk to him? I have something I'd like to give him from Tim."

She shrugged and then unlocked the door. "By the way, Tim's service was very nice." As she handed me the keychain, she added, "Please lock up once you're inside. Otherwise, people will be dropping off strays at all hours. You can leave the key with Leonard."

"Of course." Once we were in the building, I waited until Wendy drove off the premises and then motioned JP inside.

While JP remained in the lobby, Brad and I approached the grooming room. The sound of barking dogs alerted Leonard to our presence.

He glanced up from the metal table he'd just wiped down. "What are you two doing here?" He set the rag on the table's surface.

"I have a better question. How'd you get ahold of Tim's manuscript?" I extracted the pages from my tote and slapped them on the table. Brad stood by my side and glared at Leonard.

He picked up the papers. "I don't know what you're talking about," he stuttered. "This is my story. Where'd this come from?"

"You gave it to Becky."

His eyes darkened. "Yeah. So what? I wrote it. You have no way to prove otherwise."

"We have plenty of proof," Brad said. "Tim filed a copyright, and I own the rights."

As he backed toward the counter behind him, Leonard continued to stammer. "Who else knows about this?"

"For now, just us and Becky," Brad replied.

Leonard took off his glasses and polished the lenses on his t-shirt. "I have an advance and a publishing deal. This is my novel, and no one's going to take it from me." He placed his glasses back on and scowled at us. "I saw what Becky liked, and now I have it. The book, the money, and soon his home. You can't stop me."

"Becky mentioned that you're thinking about making an offer on the house. Where'd you get the funds to even consider it?" I doubted the advance was enough to cover a down payment on a house the size of Tim's.

"Let's just say I came into a little gold."

"As in treasure?" Brad asked.

Leonard shrugged.

"That was supposed to be *our* wedding present from Tim." My voice rose a few notches, and I struggled to maintain my composure. The man stole Tim's life, his story, and our wedding present, *and* he wrecked our honeymoon. I wanted to punch him.

"You people have everything." He spat the words out, his voice filled with resentment. "You have no idea what it's like to be someone like me. Tim didn't appreciate Becky. You don't deserve the treasure. Tim didn't deserve the fame and fortune, and he certainly didn't deserve Becky."

Tension radiated from Brad's body. I nudged him, and we moved in closer so that the recording device would clearly capture his answer. "So, you killed him," I said.

He sneered. "Yeah. He never saw it coming."

"You'll never get away with this." Brad raised his fist.

"Wanna bet?" Leonard lunged forward and hit Brad with the taser gun.

Brad dropped to the ground twitching.

"Brad," I gasped.

Leonard's lips upturned in a sinister grin. "You're next."

I screamed "Secret" into the mike and then swung my leg and kicked his arm with all my strength. My sneaker landed firmly on Leonard's wrist, and he released the weapon.

While I scrambled for the pistol in my tote, JP rushed into the room and pointed his gun at Leonard. "Freeze."

Leonard's eyes darted around the place as he searched for an escape. I prepared to pounce, while Brad attempted to recover from the shock of the taser.

After a long tense minute, Leonard's shoulders slumped. He raised his arms in the air.

JP tossed me the cuffs and then began to read him his rights. After I cuffed Leonard, I muttered, "I hope you rot in jail." Then I bent down and helped Brad up.

Once Brad found his footing, he gripped JP's shoulder and shook his hand. "Thanks, man."

"De rien. I am glad you are all right, mon ami." JP replied, then alerted the cops that we'd made the arrest.

Leonard hissed. "You'll never be able to prove anything."

"Hey, Leonard." I raised my t-shirt and showed him the recording device. "Wanna bet?"

~ * ~

As Brad and I lounged on the beach behind Tim's home, I mulled over the whirlwind of events that had transpired during our trip.

When Leonard arrived at the station, Aaron booked him for murder. The evidence was rock solid. Leonard broke down and admitted he'd followed Tim home from Becky's apartment. While Tim unpacked, Leonard snuck up from behind, tased him, and then administered the fatal drug. He snatched the treasure map off the nightstand, wrapped Tim in a tablecloth, and threw his body in the trunk of his car. Then he went back inside for Tim's laptop and phone. After he'd picked the locks of the desk drawers and searched the office for any remaining evidence of the story, he drove home and waited until after midnight to dump Tim's body in the Caribbean Sea.

Leonard also confessed that he'd followed Tim when he'd discovered the treasure. While Tim attended our wedding, Leonard dug up the loot and hauled the chest of coins away. In hopes of a lighter sentence, he revealed where the goods were stored. The Cayman Islands National Museum would take possession of the gold.

Becky had another one of her meltdowns when she'd heard the news of Leonard's arrest. Her dreams of an escape from the bank teller business through a rich husband were destroyed . . . for now. With Leonard and Tim out of the picture, I wondered if she'd continue to pursue a relationship with Aaron. To top it off, Spencer, her mentor and protector, was under investigation for his role in the money laundering scheme. When I'd called to say goodbye, she said that the bank swarmed with financial forensic auditors collecting evidence. She struggled to meet the demands of her job while satisfying the auditors' requests.

When I asked her what would happen to the shelter with Leonard in jail, she explained that one of the volunteers recently retired from his job as a teacher. He'd cover Leonard's duties until a replacement was hired. All the workers would put in extra hours to aid in the transition. As we ended the call, she'd asked to stay in touch.

When I responded, "Of course." Duke yipped.

Yesterday, Lawson, Jenny, Brad, and I paid a visit to Pearl.

We arrived mid-morning, ahead of the lunch crowd. After the introductions to our friends, Pearl poured each of us a cup of Jamaican Blue Coffee. She set a pitcher of creamer and a bowl of sugar on the kitchen table.

As I poured cream into my mug, Pearl explained the reason for Jax's father's stoic demeanor. "Jax's dad found out his boy told yer friend 'bout his business cleaning da money. Don't ask me how. Meybe dat dirty cop. Rumor has it, he knew dey gonna kill his son, but did nuttin. So sad," she sighed.

"How awful." I took a sip of the smooth brew. "Does his wife know?"

"Dat woman. She be in denial." Pearl shook her head. "Let's talk 'bout something else."

Jenny beamed as Pearl divulged that her Granny many generations ago was Blackbeard's girlfriend. The directions to Edward's treasure had been passed down over the years. Our brilliant friend Tim had been the first to make the connections and find the buried goods.

My heart melted when Brad extracted the gold coin from his pocket and placed it in Pearl's hand. As tears of joy streamed down her cheeks, I etched the memory in my brain. The image would be one of a handful of my own treasures from this honeymoon from hell.

We joined the lunch crowd and devoured some of Pearl's brown chicken stew and then danced to Jams's tunes. After an hour, we reluctantly said goodbye to our new friends and headed back to the house. Jenny and Lawson needed to pack for their flight back to Charleston. I prayed Snooper and Irish would adjust well to their new home.

When Brad left to drive them to the airport, Duke sat by the door and whined. Our dog would miss his buddies.

JP and Brad had exchanged contact information and were now texting on a regular basis about the upcoming World Cup. JP believed France would take the trophy. Brad was betting on Ireland. As I reflected on their first encounter, I thanked God for that outcome.

Another welcome surprise was that I now considered Aaron a friend. I added him to my list of colleagues that I could consult with when I needed advice.

The pest control company would arrive tomorrow to extract the bats. In two days, we'd leave for Tim's memorial service in California.

Brad interrupted my train of thought when he leaned over and gave me one of his toe-tingling kisses. We planned to make the most of every moment of our last days on the island.

Acknowledgements

I'm always amazed when I finish a story. There were moments when the plot escaped me and moments of synchronicity. I'm so grateful for all the support I had along the way. Thank you Lord for the inspiration for the stories and the faith to carry it through. And thank you to my family and friends, most especially my husband, Barry, who bears through the ups and downs with me.

A special shoutout to John Cassara for his invaluable expertise on money laundering. His generosity with his time and knowledge were priceless. He's written multiple books on the subject, and he spent a career bringing justice to money laundering thieves. If you're curious about the subject, I highly recommend reading his books. John Cassara

Thanks to our friends, Tim Scanlan and Julie Cole, for scouting Grand Cayman for me on their recent trip. Although I've been to the island, it's been a few years. Tim is also one of my beta readers. He played a huge part in the believability of the plot. I can't thank him enough.

I'd also like to thank our friend, David Dettling, who offered his expertise in the death care industry.

A huge shoutout to my beta readers including John, Tricia, Chris, Mary Ellen, Kimberly, Eileen, and Tim. Your feedback was invaluable.

I am grateful to be part of an author community. Big thanks to Tricia T. LaRochelle, Lou Kemp, the Mystery Review Crew, and the League of Romance Writers, all of whom have been very supportive. I'd also like to thank Dr. Bernadette Anderson, Eileen Joyce-Donovan, Mare Galeos, and Ani Tuzman, otherwise known as the 'Sassies.' I think of you all every time I release a book. It's hard to believe it's been a few years since we all sat around the dining table at the bed and breakfast in Vermont. I remember the belly laughs and our pledge to publish our works no matter what.

It takes a village to produce a book. Many thanks to my cover designer, Brandi Doane McCann, my editing team at Lone Star Literary Life, my proofreader, Susan Fegraeus, and the folks at Literary Titan.

A special thanks to our friend, Jack McCloskey, for his spot-on feedback on the cover and cover copy and to the crew at Finn McCool's Irish pub for their support. A shoutout as well to Fe for her ideas that enhanced the cover.

And last, but most importantly, a big thank you to my readers. I couldn't exist without you. My mission is to deliver a good story to each of you and also benefit a larger community. I donate a portion of the proceeds from the books to causes that help the homeless, both people and pets.

If you enjoyed the story, please spread the word, and leave a rating or review. Click here for more books in the series. <u>Liz Adams Mysteries</u>

Keep turning the pages for Liz's recipes, a playlist, and a sample from the next book in the series, a novella, *A Camping Conundrum.*

Many thanks and happy reading!

All the best,

Stacy Wilder

Pearl's Jerk Chicken

Serves 8-10

Ingredients for the rice:

1 teaspoon fresh grated garlic

1 teaspoon grated fresh ginger

2 cups basmati rice

2 tablespoons butter

3 cups chicken broth

Salt and pepper to taste

1 teaspoon lime zest

Melt butter in a large saucepan and add garlic, ginger, salt, and pepper. Cook until fragrant. Add the chicken broth. Bring to a boil. Stir in rice. Cover and simmer over low heat for thirty minutes, stirring occasionally until the rice is tender, and the liquid is absorbed. When finished, stir in lime zest.

Ingredients for Chicken and Sauce:

1 rotisserie chicken

6 green onions chopped - separate the white from the green (use the green for garnish)

1/2 teaspoon scotch bonnet pepper sauce

1 teaspoon fresh grated garlic

1 teaspoon fresh grated ginger

1/4 cup chicken broth (you will need more later)

1/2 teaspoon allspice

1 teaspoon fresh minced thyme

2 tablespoons butter

1 tablespoon soy sauce

1 tablespoon white wine vinegar

1 teaspoon jerk seasoning

Pepper to taste (no need for salt)

1 teaspoon brown sugar

Juice from one lime

Smoked paprika

While the rice cooks, shred the chicken, cover, and set to the side.

In a large skillet, over medium heat melt butter, sauté garlic, onion whites, and ginger until onions are slightly soft. Add chicken broth, soy sauce, white wine vinegar, allspice, scotch bonnet sauce, jerk seasoning, pepper, and thyme. Once simmering, stir in brown sugar. Allow to slightly thicken and then add lime juice.

Add shredded chicken and stir to coat. Slowly add chicken broth until the mixture reaches a stew-like consistency.

Serve on top of rice. Sprinkle smoked paprika on the chicken and garnish with tops of green onions.

Enjoy!

Pearl's Kickin' Beans

Serves 8-10

Ingredients:

Two 15 ounce cans of ranch style beans (with juice)

1 teaspoon scotch bonnet pepper sauce

1/2 teaspoon powdered garlic

Two slices hickory-smoked bacon

Salt and pepper to taste

In a large saucepan, combine the above ingredients. Cover and heat on medium heat for fifteen to twenty minutes.

Liz's Mango Margaritas

Serves 4

Ingredients:

2-3 ripe mangos chopped into cubes

2-3 tablespoons agave syrup

½ cup Blanco Tequila

¼ cup lime juice

2 tablespoons Cointreau

A pinch of salt

3 cups ice

Puree mango in blender. Add remaining ingredients and blend on high until smooth.

Enjoy!

Liz's Roasted Veggies

Serves 8-10

Ingredients:

4 carrots

1 head of cauliflower

1 head of broccoli

Coconut oil

Juice from one lime

Preheat oven to 450 degrees. Peel and slice carrots into ¼ inch rounds. Trim and cut broccoli and cauliflower into bite-sized pieces. Place cut vegetables in a roasting pan and toss with a generous drizzle of coconut oil. Season with salt and pepper. Roast for twenty minutes or until veggies are lightly browned and tender. Toss with lime juice and serve.

Enjoy!

Ida's Key Lime Cookies

Makes two dozen cookies

Ingredients:

1 ½ cups of flour

½ teaspoon baking powder

¼ teaspoon baking soda

¼ teaspoon sea salt

3 tablespoons freshly grated lime zest

1 cup sugar

1 teaspoon vanilla

1 stick softened butter

2 tablespoons plain Greek yogurt

4 teaspoons lime juice

Preheat oven to 350 degrees. In a bowl, whisk flour, baking soda, baking powder, and sea salt together. In a separate mixing bowl, add sugar and lime zest. Add softened butter to the sugar mixture and whisk until light and airy. Add yogurt, vanilla, and lime juice. Fold in the flour mixture. Place the cookie dough in the fridge for at least fifteen minutes. Form the dough into small balls. Place on a greased cookie sheet leaving at least two inches of space between each cookie. Bake for twelve minutes or until crispy at the edges and then let the cookies sit for five minutes before serving.

Enjoy!

The Cayman

Conundrum Playlist:

1. "I Hope You Dance," Lee Ann Womack and Sons of the Desert
2. "What A Wonderful World," Louis Armstrong
3. "What A Feeling," Irene Cara
4. "Conga," Gloria Estefan and Miami Sound Machine
5. "Vacation," The Go-Go's
6. "Kokomo," The Beach Boys
7. "Who Let the Dogs Out," Baha Men
8. "Tell It Like It is," Aaron Neville
9. "Jamming," Bob Marley and The Wailer's
10. "Rock the Boat," The Hues Corporation
11. "Don't Worry, Be Happy," Bobby McFerrin

12. "Day-O (The Banana Boat Song)," Harry Belafonte
13. "Amazing Grace," Il Divo
14. "One Sweet Day," Maraih Carey, Boyz II Men
15. "Three Little Birds," Bob Marley and the Wailers
16. "This Kiss," Faith Hill

A sneak peek at . . .

A Camping Conundrum

As I applied a coat of mascara to my lashes, I wondered why I'd let my husband talk me into sleeping on the hard ground in a tent. I shuddered at the possible creepy crawlies that might join us. At first I'd said no. The look on his crestfallen face softened my better judgement. When he shared fond memories of his family camp trips to Poinsett Park, I caved.

Brad lost both his sister and his parents to separate tragic accidents. Who was I to deprive him of reliving his cherished childhood experiences?

When I changed my answer, a big grin spread across his face. "There are bike trails, a lake to swim in, plenty of birds, and flora and fauna. Duke will love it."

Yeah. Our Labrador retriever would have a blast, but what about me? I hated to camp. The reason why rushed back as I recalled that fateful night.

As a Girl Scout, I couldn't wait to add the coveted camping badge to my collection. I piled into the van with eleven other eager ten-year old girls and two counselors. As the counselor drove us to campgrounds just outside of Atlanta, we chattered and giggled. After we unloaded the van, we set up our tents. My tent mate and I struggled with the poles and then finally claimed success. By dinner time, we were starving. Our troop collected logs, built a fire, and cooked a feast of hot dogs and baked beans. As a magical golden Georgia moon rose, we sang campfire songs and roasted marshmallows. My tastebuds tingled at the recollection of the smores and the melted chocolate that oozed out the sides.

When dark set in, the idyllic scene took a turn. Two men with pantyhose pulled over their heads appeared out of nowhere. I closed my eyes as I remembered the horror of their smushed faces. Waving knives, they demanded that the counselors give them money and food. They took off with the goods, and the adults ushered us into the van while they waited for the cops. The sound of sobs filled the space, and I couldn't stop shaking. Because we never completed the trip, I never earned that badge . . . and I never went camping again.

I shook my head and attempted to eradicate the memory. If worse came to worse, I suppose I could always hole up in the sprinter van that Brad had gifted me as a wedding present. I sighed in resignation, then rose from my vanity table and exchanged my robe for a black camisole and jeans. Once I completed the ensemble with a black lace shrug, I slipped into a pair of cream-colored espadrilles. I added silver hoop earrings and spritzed my neck with my favorite perfume, Amazing Grace.

Once a month, the women in our neighborhood gathered for an evening of fun and friendly competition. Tonight, my next-door neighbor Maria was hosting a karaoke competition combined with a Cabi clothing line shopping event.

One of her coworkers, Michelle, recently left the shipping company where they both worked to become a full-time Cabi stylist. Maria wanted to support her efforts. I'd deliberately chosen my outfit to make it easy to try on the merchandise.

Brad and Duke were settled on the couch in the living room watching a baseball game. When the doorbell rang, our dog hopped off and made a beeline for the door.

"I'll get it." I held Duke's collar and exchanged the pizza for the cash Brad had left on the front table. Duke's tail swished at the smell of pepperoni.

After I placed the pizza in the kitchen for the boys, I grabbed the bouquet of flowers I'd bought for Maria, kissed Brad goodbye, and headed next door.

~ * ~

"Liz, come in." Maria accepted the package of parrot tulips in varying shades of orange and fuchsia. "Thank you. You didn't need to do this. Follow me. Everyone's in the kitchen."

"You're welcome," I said as I trailed after her.

While Maria placed the flowers in a vase, I joined the women gathered around the center island. Spring rolls, egg rolls, a Chinese chicken salad, wontons, and various sauces were spread over the island countertop.

"What are you going to sing?" my neighbor, Linda, asked.

"Haven't decided yet. You?" I placed a spring roll and an egg roll on a paper plate and added a generous dollop of hot mustard. The spicy sauce was bound to clear out my sinuses.

"O Canada." Linda winked. Since she was originally from there, I'm sure she knew the song by heart.

"Everyone, please load up your plates and grab a seat in the living room. Michelle is ready to get started," Maria announced.

I added some citrus chicken salad with crunchy noodles to my plate and then helped myself to a glass of sauvignon blanc. Once everyone was seated, Michelle introduced herself. A long rack of clothes blocked the view of Maria's fireplace. Michelle passed out pens and catalogs that contained descriptions of each item.

"Mark what you like as I go," she said. "There will be time to try the pieces on afterward, and I'm happy to answer any questions on sizes." After we went around the room and introduced ourselves, Michelle asked, "Does anyone have an upcoming trip?"

I groaned. "I'm going camping in two weeks." My sixty-two year old neighbor, Cassie, gave me a puzzled look. "Brad talked me into it," I explained.

"Oh, I have just the collection for that! I was going to start with Spring Luxe, instead I'll start with Summer Fun. Get your pen ready, Liz."

As Michelle showcased each section of the catalog, she pointed out trends and different pieces that paired well together.

Afterward we all tried on clothes, and I ended up purchasing four T-shirts, a skort, two pairs of shorts, and a windbreaker. I couldn't resist throwing in a pair of dangly earrings. As Michelle added up my total, she assured me that the order would arrive in time for my trip.

"Time for karaoke," Maria announced. We reconvened in the living room, and she explained the rules. "We'll start out with two teams. Liz, Michelle, and I will be Team One. Cassie, Gwen, and Linda, you'll be Team Two." She cleared her throat and continued, "For the first round, everyone will sing one song. Then the other team will decide who to eliminate from the opposing team. Any questions so far?"

Maria passed out the list of song choices. I caught a frown on Linda's face and then noticed that "O Canada" wasn't on the list.

No one had questions, and Maria resumed the instructions. "After a second song, the eliminated players will judge which two singers move on to the final round. The winner will get a fifty dollar gift card and second place a twenty-five dollar gift card." She held up the prizes. "Someone from Team One will sing first, followed by someone from Team Two. Ladies, get ready!"

Since we'd all had a few glasses of wine, this would be fun.

"Liz, you're up." Maria handed me the microphone, and I crooned B-52s "Love Shack." Not an easy song with both the male and female parts, but I thought I nailed it. My quiet librarian neighbor Gwen followed. She shocked the crowd with a rendition of "These Boots are Made for Walkin'" by Nancy Sinatra. Dang, Gwen was in it to win it. After everyone finished, the teams voted. Linda and Maria were eliminated.

Michelle started round two with "Crazy," by Patsy Cline. I botched Pat Benatar's "Hit Me with Your Best Shot." Cassie ended with a pitch-perfect "I Will Survive" by Gloria Gaynor. Michelle and I were eliminated. Maria called a break before the champion session between Cassie and Gwen began.

We all whooped and hollered as the final round started. Cassie took the mike first and belted out, "The Lady is a Tramp," by Ella Fitzgerald. She sashayed as she sang. Since Cassie's nickname was Sassy Cassie, it was the perfect song. Gwen followed with a mesmerizing performance of Julie Andrew's "My Favorite Things." Gwen won hands down.

It was past midnight when I stumbled home with a much better attitude about the upcoming camping trip. After all, I was a big girl now. I'd be there with my husband and our dog. We'd have the sprinter van, and I'd be dressed to the nines. What could possibly go wrong?